Fire in May

Fire in May

Victoria Lopez

TATE PUBLISHING
AND ENTERPRISES, LLC

Published by Tate Publishing & Enterprises, LLC
127 E. Trade Center Terrace | Mustang, Oklahoma 73064 USA
1.888.361.9473 | www.tatepublishing.com

Tate Publishing is committed to excellence in the publishing industry. The company reflects the philosophy established by the founders, based on Psalm 68:11,

"The Lord gave the word and great was the company of those who published it."

Book design copyright © 2016 by Tate Publishing, LLC. All rights reserved.
Cover design by Joshua Rafols
Art by Victoria Lopez
Interior design by Manolito Bastasa
Author head shot by Arthur Bryan Marroquin/ABM Photography

Published in the United States of America

ISBN: 978-1-68270-647-3
Fiction / General
15.12.17

1

I DIDN'T WANT to leave. Anywhere else I could go would only leave me longing for the places I had been, for the person I had become. I had been enlightened; they couldn't forcefully remove me from the place in which I had come to find solitude, where I had finally found peace after all the years of agony. It had been as though my insides were set afire, yet no sensation of pain was present. There was no discomfort, no yearning to evade the flames, which were presumably swallowing me whole. When they stole me away from the dancing light that warmed my aching soul, that's when the heaviness of my reality suffocated me. I had found refuge in this new place. I wandered aimlessly with no direction, yet I followed a distinctive path. I had always been lost. Lost in imagination, lost in day dreams, lost in hopelessness—a lost cause; I had nowhere to go, no one to go to. They said I was loved, that they would take care of me, but I had never believed them. They only wanted to take away my fire. It was mine. It found me when I was alone, and when I told it that I wanted to be alone, it knew I was lying.

No one else knew when I was lying. They would say, "You are so strong, you are doing so well. You are fearless." I'd lie to them all the time. I'd nod my head and blink my long, brown eyelashes. They fell for it each time, every time, and I made a game of it. I'd take their compliments, and they would think that I believed them. I didn't though. I am smart, a clever girl; I was not strong, the fire was. I was not doing well; the fire made me well. And although I like to lie, I like to play games, I will say the truth in this: I did believe when they called me fearless because of the many things I am not, one thing I undoubtedly was, was fearless.

This was new. I had come to understand that fear only made me more clever. I rather enjoyed being clever and rather disliked being afraid. Many nights I would lay awake, afraid—afraid of nothing, afraid of everything. I'd turn around before closing my bedroom door to make sure they weren't going to sneak in behind me. As I lay in bed praying for rest to come, I'd open my eyes and search the corners of the room; they prefer dark, high corners. From there they can watch, observe while remaining unseen, unnoticed, yet somehow I am fully aware of their presence. A bump from a dark corner, a creak at the end of the hallway, a heavy sigh beside my ear, the sound of my sheets rustling against one another as I desperately searched for a comfortable position to hold myself in bed. Sometimes, as I lay uncomfortably in bed, my tongue would become dry with thirst. This obtuse need to leave the safe dwelling of my sheeted shelter was an essential human requirement that longed to be satisfied; the curiosity was the sole cause of my unsettled demeanor. Perhaps I could not rest until I provided my tongue with just a taste of what it longed for. Perhaps what I longed for was not of this world, but of another that has yet to be poisoned by man's hand. Such implications only fueled my yearning, my human curiosity.

I always considered this urge to confront the line that separated my bed from the shadows a challenge. Slowly I'd untangle myself from my red sheets, and I'd dare the shadowed line to approach me. Boldly, I'd whisper valiant declarations of urgent necessity toward the ambient sense of an omniscient presence. And I could almost surely promise you, I would receive an echoed mutter, which would resound off the walls of my home and set fire to my chilled veins.

I woke up wide-eyed, and soaked in sweat, with my heart pounding heavily through a heaving chest. I blinked rapidly, trying to gain awareness of my surroundings. Everything was as it had always been—unchanged and untouched. Slowly, I pulled myself into a seated position and leaned against my plush, patterned pillows. The back of my neck rested against the cold, black metal frame of my detailed headboard. The contrast of its freezing temperature in comparison to my smoldering body heat slightly stung. Another sleepless night. I had grown accustomed to nights such as these——,nights spent in fear and anxiety of an unseen entity. I suppose I evaded their influence once more. Silence was ever-present, an unusual happening in my home, which was typically filled with conversation. I turned my body toward the edge of my bed cautiously. Perhaps I was alone. Perhaps the absence of company was necessary. With a tentative sigh, I leaned my head back and stretched. My body has grown tired. Not due to exertion; no, in fact, I had rested well. Bedridden. There has been no medical diagnosis; there is no medical diagnosis. To call it depression would be a weak man's assumption; to recognize it as an oncoming fever would be a concerned mother's worry. I do not wish to portray myself as one suffering of physical degradation; that is not the case. See, I am anguished by the human condition. It is the hypochondriac that hopes for resolve through medication, and I, well, I do not have such luxury. To lay back with eyes closed shut is to surrender to the human condition. My only solace, the only sure way to secure my survival, is to actively seek that which will set my soul ablaze, to awake the purpose that remains dormant in this body my soul has ached to comprehend. Medication would be lovely, but life truly lived will be all the lovelier.

Resolve through rest would be the acceptance of my spirit's death, and she is one I dare not live without.

There was something eerie, something unknown, drawing my attention toward my door. It was as though an invisible line was pulling my soul through my body toward an energy that I did not understand, that I could perhaps not understand. I did not want to accept this invitation, yet this urge to comply was unsettling; it devoured me. My curiosity was immense, my sense of fear undaunted. My being, my entire self was drawn to this sensation, this unknown spirit, and to its call, I answered.

My bare feet stood solid against the wooden floor. Inching toward the doorway, arm extended to turn the brass knob, I took a long sigh. With a swift motion—nothing, no one, alone. I turned to look up the staircase. Fifteen steps to the second floor. Whatever it may be, it is luring me in that direction. Instinctively I followed this unheard beckon. Standing at the edge of the staircase, I looked up and saw nothing, heard nothing, yet still and stronger yet I was being coaxed toward this anonymity. As I ascended toward this promising omniscient presence, doubt overwhelmed my entirety.

Am I as fearless as I believe myself to be? As I take each step toward the unknown, will I find myself further lost in regret? Life has not been fair, nor has it been particularly unfair. To question such unfamiliar sentiments—shouldn't

I be thrilled, exhilarated? I had become accustomed to routine, to the ordinary, to what has been deemed as normality. I have lived with blind eyes, tired eyes yet still and ever so, rarely could they find rest. With eyes open, perhaps that is when I have been most asleep, most unaware of what truly has surrounded me throughout my unaccomplished time inhaling selfish amounts of filthy air. No, I choose to be awake; I choose to be alive. Boldly, fearlessly, I continued climbing the stairs to find that I was no longer in a familiar setting. What is this place?

2

AS I LOOKED at my surroundings, it became clear to me that I was no longer where I was and I was never going to be where I had been. There was nothing, but vast space, complete unknown that stretched for miles. Nothing contained this space; I could not think of anything that could possibly even attempt to contain it. It was unbound and limitless. I was lost, not in fear or in skepticism, but in its wonder. It was then, in that moment, that I realized that this was simply the beginning of something that I may never understand, and I accepted that. I accepted the fact that I may never understand why I was here or what my purpose was; I was merely thankful for such an experience. This, how profound—it could not be captured, could not be contained; it could only be experienced, and no fear could steal such wonder.

I absorbed everything in sight in wide-eyed marvel. My pupils fully dilated; the room's lighting was difficult to adjust to. I stood in the middle of what seemed to be an abandoned warehouse of a dilapidated factory. It was overtaken by rust, left to deteriorate. There was no evidence left of what used to be built, no reminisce of the hands that created in this space. It was haunting, mesmerizing, and the room smelled of oil and grease. There were large I-beams—those used for building skyscrapers—scattered on the floor. Nuts and bolts were left untouched in piles on the maintenance lines. There was no one to be seen and, eerily, nothing to be heard. The faint sound of an accelerated heartbeat could be heard through my chest. I was cold, still wearing the cotton nightdress I had woken up in. My feet had a layer of dirt and history on their heels.

I mouthed assurance to myself as I wandered this place, this new dimension. How did I come to be here? Why? Must I fuss with the details? Should I fuss? No. My composure was pinnacle. Of the many things I had come to expect of this life, skipping time or space travel had by no means reached the forefront. What I was experiencing, this place that I had come to be in, I had no name to call it. There was no reference to make or lesson to be recalled. All I could do was remain calm and seek a way through.

I stumbled forward, keeping eye on the ground on which I stepped, taking note of every detail that did not hide in dust and cobweb. I was alone; there seemed to be no life in this space, yet there was history—there had been life.

Perhaps there had once been a society, perhaps it was lost, perhaps it was stolen, but it was no longer thriving. I forced my eyes to focus in the dim light; its source was unknown. There were no windows, no vents, no doors, no steps—no hope. Did they engulf into nothingness? Were they swallowed by monotony? Who were they and where had they gone, and if they went, was it by choice? There must have been fear if evacuation was made by force, but there was no evidence of struggle. I circled the warehouse; no exit was to be found, but I was determined. The way that I had come was no longer available to me; I could not backtrack, and I was forced to move forward. I continued in circles, wandering the various workstations, and when I was beginning to lose faith in my previous choices, when I was unsure of where I was going, in the dust engraved, I found, "If you have gone where you have always been, you will never find where you must be." I stared. They were gone, but their lesson, their story, was not. It was not dead, it was in me, and I, well, I did not intend to fall victim.

My fingers longed to trace their forgotten message, but I dared not touch that which had already been lost. I understood that I knew very little, and knowing very little made me small. I continued to wander through the warehouse, and I caught sight of my own reflection. How tired I looked. Brown eyes with gray shadows to highlight the inescapable exhaustion and lips with questions hanging from the corners. My eyes, my dark eyelashes always fluttering, always rushing to focus my vision so that I could see more clearly. I was in fair health, but my heart was weak, my character weak, and my entirety was weak. I had always felt as though my soul was meant for another body—a body more able to hold it in place—but, no, my petite frame allowed each grand triviality to spill all about me. It had worried me so—the idea of losing myself to this earth that seemed to thrive on loss—I had no desire to feed that which had only stolen and starved those who had given it everything.

Forward I went, looking more diligently now for a way out. I had been making circles, going around; I would find my steps in the dust. I was never worried. My steps seemed confident. I should be frightened, I should be filled with anxiety; my steps were confident, I was not alone. I had myself for company, yes; I have always had myself, and I will always have myself. Unless I became lost. Yes, perhaps I would become lost and then, only then, would I truly know loneliness. That was not a burden I should carry though. Of the many things I could lose, the saddest loss of all would be the loss of myself, and the worst part, the most devastating part, is that I could only lose myself to myself. I was still searching for a way out of this dim warehouse; there seemed to be no exit, and I was now talking aloud to myself.

"It would be quite funny, wouldn't it be? Perhaps not funny, maybe ironic. Yes! It would be ironic. Ironic if I lost myself when the only company to be had was myself. Oh, look at me, look at me wandering while wondering. I refuse to be lost. I haven't an idea where I am."

I would speak out loud and hear the echo of my sure voice resonate throughout the warehouse. My hands now were grazing the broken equipment, my fingers running lines through the gathered dust. At one point I stopped and traced my initials, MW, into the dust that was left. It was then that I noticed something was trailing me; something was following me. I could not make sense of what it was, but it was animal-like, made up of the darkest darkness, the blackest of blacks, and it set fire to my bones. Chills were running rabid in my blood; for the first time during this journey to nowhere, I was frightened. I was shaken, unsure, and immense doubt flooded my being. I had seen this presence before. I know that it had always seen me. I began to walk more quickly; I kept my steps confident. How did it find me in this place? Had it always been here, or had it come along with me? No, it lived in high corners and behind open doors. It lived in the darkness and swallowed the light. Two, four, six. Two, four, six.

It swept behind the dilapidated steel bars and crouched. It kneeled there, looking through the gaps that allowed vision. It did not care to be hidden; it wanted to be seen but not known. It did not want to be understood. Mystery evoked fear and revelation; revelation alleviated fear. It swayed as though it was preparing to pounce, but I knew it wouldn't; it never had before. It simply provoked me with its presence, and it had no other intention but that. I thought that I had rid myself of him. He had been gone for so long—for so long—but now, now he sits with me in this doorless room. Two, four, six. Two, four, six. I did as I had done before.

"I do not accept you. Begone, begone and return to your death. I do not welcome you, you are not welcome here!" I twisted my body in quick circles, I felt as though I was surrounded. The dry air was no longer filling my lungs.

My declaration was one of confidence, yet my body language contradicted every breath. My nerves were anxious, and my eyes ran wildly around the room. "I do not accept you, and you are not welcome. I am my own, and never will I be lost to you. You are already lost, and I shall not be made lost by the lost." He darted past me, around me; I would lose sight of him and only knew his presence by the sound of his claws scraping against the concrete floor of the warehouse. What is this and why has it begun again? Again.

I closed my eyes tightly, shutting out my unknown surroundings, and allowed myself a moment of peace. Peace had always been foreign to me. I felt as though it evaded me, I felt as though it believed me to be unworthy. Two, four, six. I opened my eyes. My surroundings were still, silent, and the same. I was alone now. He must have left, proud that he still had the same effect on me. Before I moved forward, I took a breath. What a life this is—a continuous adventure—and I, so small, could still cast a large shadow. Perhaps that is why I have found this place. Peace is not granted; it is attained through the many times that we do become lost. Only when we are lost can we be found. I was most certainly lost, and I had the most certain of hopes that I too would be found.

It was then that I looked at my surroundings once again, vast and unknown, and now at the very end of the warehouse was a way out. I wandered toward the exit, a ladder leaning upon the wall that ended on the edge of a concrete tunnel. I had no doubt; I kept my steps confident. I looked down at my feet, and a mouse scurried by. How strange. She stopped and turned back at me as though she was reassuring me that the tunnel was safe, as though she had made the journey herself. I stood at the foot of the ladder and looked up; the climb was not at all intimidating, and I took my first step. I climbed and continued to climb, and I did not think about how far I had climbed. Finally, I was sitting on the edge of the concrete tunnel, and I dared to look out to see where I had been. Yes, it was a warehouse, and it seemed as though it had once been occupied, but that must had been quite some time ago.

The tunnel was narrow but allowed enough body room to crawl comfortably on hand and knee. I moved forward, always forward. There was a lovely smell in the air, and I did not know where it came from. The tunnel seemed to narrow out, and I had to lay my body against the ground and pull myself forward. There was a dim light ahead, and finally I had reached what seemed to be the tunnel's end. I peeked out. Empty. No one was to be seen, nothing to be heard. I pulled myself through, and I was now in a new place.

3

———— ✺ ————

W HAT A LOVELY place it was too. The furnish-
ings were rich, and the ambiance was that of
poise and quality. I seemed to be in a hallway of a lavish home. The walls were cream-colored and
lined with paintings of landscapes and shapes that I did
not quite understand. Each piece was hung in a differently
styled frame that was of the same shade of gold. The floor
was a deep mahogany, waxed and shined and untarnished.
A beautiful hallway carpet, most likely Turkish, was laid
over the rich wood; it had beautiful tones of red and gold
with touches of black. That lovely smell was still lingering
in the air, and I still did not know where it came from.
It was quiet, but I could hear the faintest sound of music
playing. I was cold. My cotton nightdress was not suitable
for this environment, and I began to feel naked. I put my
focus elsewhere. Where was this smell coming from, and

that music, where did it lead? Intuitively, I followed where my intuition lead me.

I closed my eyes and took a deep breath. Two, four, six. I did not know what was to come, and I was sure that whatever my expectations could be, that they would be surpassed. I stared down the length of the hallway. What a magnificent sight it was. I could hear the distant music; I stepped closer to the wall on the right and leaned my ear against it. Yes, there was certainly music. I continued to walk forward, keeping my ear on the wall. Perhaps ten steps ahead, I could begin to hear that the music was growing in tone and volume. I pulled away from the wall and caught sight of a particular painting that was mounted for display. It was of a woman looking away and facing the cliffs edge; I suppose she might have felt alone, but maybe she had more company than most. The cliff's edge—how easy she could slip away from the troubles of the world. I found her to be courageous—silent yet poignant. I understood how she felt—alone yet accompanied by the entire world. Longing for escape yet craving life all the more. I pulled my concentration away from the painting and noticed the door on my right. I leaned my ear against it and heard a room full of music. The lovely smell sat overwhelmingly in the air, and I felt my stomach empty.

I grabbed hold of the door handle and turned it around. It was unlocked. I pushed it in, and the music came bursting through the door. I blinked my eyes and looked around the edge. There were people sitting around a table set with tea. The colors were nothing more than pastel: pinks, blues, greens, and yellows. They were beautiful, like living dolls. They were seated around the table sipping on tea with their backs straight and chins up; they were regal. The music was of a full orchestra with a sad violin solo; it seemed to be weeping, as though they were grieving an enormous loss. I was underdressed. There were three ladies and one handsome man. They were dressed in the most fashionable of Renaissance clothing in the loveliest shades of pastel and white lace. Their faces were painted as though they were of the most exquisite of their class. White powdered faces and lips of rose pink.

The lovely smell, I looked about the room; it was filled with the freshest of flowers, all so beautiful. White peonies, blue forget-me-nots, and there were species of flowers I could not name and could only admire all lined up along the walls, stunningly displayed. I went unnoticed. I walked closer to the flowers, gently grazing the tip of a white peony. This room was an atrium, with high white walls and the sun shining through the clear glass ceiling. The music overwhelmed me; I looked at all the beauty that surrounded me, yet my soul ached. My lungs were filled with the perfumes of the earth and my heart with sadness. How could sadness exist when such beauty was present? I began to walk through the aisles of greenery all potted in vases and in full bloom—alive. I began to hum along with the sad violinist. Legato bowing with loose vibrato, then the melody would be passed to the cello, an answer to comfort the hurt. I hummed aloud and admired the room.

"What is this we have? A visitor." I looked to my left to find one of the elegant ladies looking at me with a tilted head. I did not answer; she tilted her head the other way. "Do not be shy, pretty dear. I am just as you are." She was stunning. Tall with a thin face, full lips and eyelashes that embellished the cat shape of her blue eyes. "Does your tongue fail to work or does your mind?" she said in a tone of disdain as though I had rejected her. She stepped closer to me in a stalking, catlike manner. She pulled her attention away from me and toward the flowers I was admiring. She smelled wonderful, just as the flowers did. She was now standing behind me, and I did not allow myself to flinch. My chin was up, and I cautiously brushed the hair out of my face. She leaned her head to my ear and whispered, "Are they not beautiful?" She sent shivers down my spine; my heart raced, and I found that I could hardly resist her temptation of conversation.

She stepped away to the other side of the aisle and began to prune the leaves off the nearest flower, almost in a childlike manner. "Oh, dear, how I wish you would speak to me. It is often quite lonely here."

I took a deep breath and slowly turned to her. "I apologize if I am being rude. I am somewhat confused."

She turned to me, laughed with her heart, and enthusiastically said "Oh, but my pretty dear! Aren't we all confused? It would be rather dull to be a person who was seldom not. I am often confused, but more often I am quite lonely." She looked to the ground, then up at me with sadness in her piercing eyes. I was filled with remorse, with guilt, and the orchestra seemed to be playing louder yet. She spoke softly but firmly, "Please, do not feel pity for me; the beautiful most dislike being pitied. Not to say that I believe myself to be the most beautiful, but I quite often am or, more so, was quite often told that I was." She lifted her chin higher into the air, and the sun kissed her powdered white skin.

She swept the hair that outlined her delicate face and continued. "Allow me to apologize. I do not wish to make you uncomfortable. I have been told that I could be most intimidating. For the life of me I cannot understand such a statement. I am far from intimidating, look at me. Do I seem very intimidating to you?"

She did. She stood tall and confident; there was no doubt on her brow, yet she seemed to be aloof, pained. We looked at one another for a moment, and I felt the overwhelming need to comfort her. I did not understand where I was, much less did I know how I was to return home, but for now, I was alive, and that was all the comfort I needed; perhaps that too would comfort her.

I turned my eyes away from her. "Perhaps, do you think, you could introduce this place to me?" Her eyes lit up, and she excitedly pulled her arm though mine so that we were interlocked. "Oh, pretty dear, this is the most excitement I have had in such a long while. If you do not mind me asking, where do you think you are? What are your ideas, your opinions? Please, do tell me. I promise to listen."

I attempted a response, but she did not allow me enough time to form a complete thought. "Oh, I am quite thoughtless, aren't I? You must not have even had much time to form such a grand opinion, much less come to terms with your surroundings. Now, dear, don't think me rude. I am simply speaking from past experience. Rarely does anyone know where they are, much less where they might be going." She stopped and turned to me, as if trying to read my reaction. Does she mean to say that there have been others like me thrown into this unknown journey?

She was correct though. I had not given proper thought to my whereabouts, much less the route that would lead me home. I did not have an exact reason, an explanation; had I scorned the universe? Perhaps God? Did I upset a natural balance that I have never known that I was to respect? I supposed that I had stepped into an alternate universe, perhaps even another world. The first made much more sense to me seeing as I was home and then I was not. I was being led by an inhuman—or maybe completely human—presence that called me into this anomaly. I shook myself awake and turned my attention to the woman who had laced her arm with mine, and softly I spoke to her, "I do not know your name."

"My name?" Her eyes fell to the ground then back up, filled with tears too proud to fall. "Most will ask the names of the flowers before they would ask for mine." I could hear the pain trembling in her voice; it matched the rising vibrato of the strings. "Za'ara, my name is Za'ara."

I stood and watched her admire the many flowers that surrounded us. "Well, your name rivals the beauty of the flowers themselves."

To my compliment, Za'ara lit up. "Oh, my lovely darling! You flatter me, and I do very much enjoy it. Enough, let us continue. You have much to learn and twice as much to experience. I understand why you might be here, but I believe that you have no understanding as to why you might be here; this worries me. It worries me so."

She again looped her arm within mine and led me through the aisles of wonderfully colored flowers. I looked more closely at the flowers, taking note of their impressive stature. All were in porcelain pots, separated at the root and wonderfully delightful. With a fingertip touching the very edge of a porcelain pot, I asked, "Za'ara, are these flowers rooted, or have they been cut?" She did not look at me, but she smiled; she straightened her spine and stretched her nose higher into the air. More boldly, I spoke, "It would not make sense to me if they had been cut; flowers that have been cut of their roots only hold on to their beauty for a short period of time before they fade."

She closed her eyes for a moment and replied, "Tell me, do you believe that these flowers have been cut?"

"I do not think they have been; if they had been cut, they then would not be standing so tall and proud."

Za'ara stopped and looked at me sternly. "Listen here, beauty can rise from filth. If born from unconventional circumstance, perhaps even from brokenness, beauty can and, if truly beautiful, will stand tall and proud until it no longer can. That is what makes beauty all the more spectacular, it is what brings hope to the hopeless."

I fell silent. Za'ara held a personal stake on this particular topic. I could not determine if she related to that of the fallen beauty or of the hopeless seed who silently kept hope to one day root. Who was I to make such a judgement? She and I stood in the same place, sharing in this unknown experience, and I, in my all sincerity, believed that she might be learning just as I am, no slower nor any faster. All I could do was live and continue forth.

"Za'ara, if you could tell me one thing to be true, if you could yell down from the mountain most high, what truth would you speak to fall upon the ear of those willing to hear?"

"What a lovely thought that is, but how much more lovely is it that you need not reach the mountains most high but simply own the bravery to breathe hope into the ear merely a whisper away. That, my darling, is the lesson. The lesson that hope must be brave to stand when beauty no longer can. Beauty can be lost, but when hope is lost, beauty is nothing, and life will cease."

If I had believed that I understood before, then I was sorely mistaken. I was in awe, in awe of the dormant potential that sat on my tongue. That is the lesson. The lesson of what? Of this life, of this experience? Za'ara still has her arm laced around mine, and I could hear my heart beating louder still. The sad violin melody continued in the background, and my soul matched its rhythm. I spoke not; I had already spoken and was spoken over by a tongue sharper than my own.

4

--- ≈※≈ ---

WE CONTINUED TO walk down the aisles of flowers in silence and neared the table that I had seen when first entering the room. The lovely people were still sitting and drinking tea. As I sat in the seat, as gestured by Za'ara, I began to feel cold and uncomfortable. My cotton nightdress was not suitable attire for such a neatly displayed table, nor was I suitable to be the company of such beautiful hosts. Za'ara sat at the head of the table; the seat across from me remained empty. My lovely company had seemingly failed to notice me, and a shiver ran down my spine. The table was wonderfully decorated. The linens were lined with fine lace, and its delicate white hue draped marvelously to the ground. The ground. I had failed to notice the exquisite epoch porcelain tile that the atrium was floored in. My bare feet were soiled, and I was ashamed; I desperately wanted to wash them.

An immense sadness overcame me. My eyes searched for comfort in those of my company, but they too shared the same pained look. How have I come to be this way? I turned to the aisles of flowers; there they were, lovely and innocent. Untarnished. I only became more aware of the filth that coated my feet, and a second wave of vulnerability choked me. There had been a shift in the room's energy. Two, four, six. I breathed in deeply; yet air failed to fill my lungs. With a second sigh, I inhaled again and again and twice more, but my lungs were empty and I emptier still. Panic began to overwhelm me—no. My eyes were wide, and my heart was racing; my hand clung to the table's top, and I fought tears. Breathe. Two, four, six. I looked again to the faces of my company, and none seemed to notice my struggle. I looked to Za'ara, and her eyes found mine. She looked at me with a tilted head and wore no expression. There was no remorse, and I could not understand why she did not offer her aid. She tilted her head the other way and continued to watch me, then tucked a loose strand of hair behind her ear and placed her hands neatly on the table, all the while maintaining direct eye contact. I struggled to maintain focus; I inhaled a last attempt for air with a sharp shriek but to no avail. My vision was slipping, and my body was becoming heavy.

I thrust my head to the side and gasped for air—heaving, choking, coughing. One hand still held to the table, and the other held the chair's arm. I coughed, and something sharp cut against the inside of my throat. Tears fell from my eyes, and I brought one hand to my neck. I gagged, and this object contracted forcefully within my throat. I fought with this obstruction and with great effort fought harder still to retain consciousness. With one last effort I coughed with my entire body's might, and into my hand the obstruction was released. Perfumed air once again filled my lungs, and I weakly sat back down again into the chair. I turned to Za'ara, and still she wore no expression.

I then brought my eyes to the hand that clenched the retched object. Slowly I opened my palm, and there upon it sat a seed of fair size. I brought it closer to my eyes, and a seed it was. Oval in shape with sharp edges, brown in color toward the center, and cream at the tips. I breathed much easier now, but still I had no peace. I brought my eyes up from the seed and found that my hosts now acknowledged my presence. Their lovely faces stared at me, wearing no expression still. I placed the seed on the table in front of me, and finally Za'ara dared to speak.

"Darling child, look at your creation! I pray that it shall be lovely and bloom abundantly." Our company placed their teacups upon the table and began to clap. I did not understand what was happening. My throat still hurt, and I placed my hand upon it once more.

"Oh, yes. Yes, this is truly a moment to cherish, unless it is not. Her truth has not yet been born into this world quite yet." Za'ara then turned to the man who sat next to the empty chair before me. "Go now. Gather the cart and apparatus." The handsome man nodded his head and stood up. His pale blue eyes stared into mine, and then he turned to leave. The others sat silently at the table and blinked. The handsome man in the pale green pants returned pushing a silver cart. He parked it, and Za'ara then gestured to the table, and he came to it and placed a teacup and plate in front of me. He gently grabbed the teapot and poured a serving. He, like the others, wore no expression, and all I could find in his eyes was a slight of sadness. He turned away and sat back into his seat; not again did he look at me.

Za'ara stood and made graceful circles around the cart. On it sat a porcelain white pot much like the others that I had seen earlier. Her finger again found the edge of the rim, and she gently grazed it with much longing. I looked again at my seed.

"Drink now. Your throat must still ache from the delivery. I know you must have many questions, but we must hurry now. The storm of absolution is nearly upon us, and we must not have your soul's seed become tainted."

My—I did as she asked and drank the tea without question. Although I knew not its contents, I believed that no harm would come to me. I wiped my lips with the back of my hand and stood. I picked up my seed with my thumb and index finger and brought it above my head to the light. My soul's seed. It looked rather ordinary, like that of a mighty oak but ordinary all the same. I held it tightly in my hand and approached Za'ara. The temperature of the atrium dropped, and a heavy wind began to echo within the room's walls.

"Za'ara, what did you mean when you said that I cannot allow my soul's seed to become tainted? How did this seed come to be inside of me?"

She furrowed her brow and raised her voice over the wind that was growing stronger yet and replied, "Sweet child, how can you have seen all that you have and still be so blind? You are a seed of the earth and have been sown to reap. Does a seed not multiply? It is our response to circumstance that defines us. Our heart may lead us and whisper hope internally, but it is our actions that truly speak volumes. Have you kept all that is beautiful within you? Have you been selfish and vain? Darling child, do you breathe hope into the ear merely a whisper away? Or must you climb to the mountains most high and call the attention of others upon yourself? Your soul's seed is a reflection of your spirit in a malleable, natural form. Though here, the same principles do not necessarily apply. You will be exposed to many who wish to taint your spirit, and those many have been many times successful. You must divulge into the parts of yourself that you might not recognize; you must accept them or you will be lost."

For a moment, I recalled all that I had encountered throughout this journey, this escapade to further unknown. I have, for the most part, been able to encounter these supernatural oddities with grace, and although I have been speculative, I have managed to accept all without excessive dispute. Za'ara had spoken of the need for hope. Perhaps I needed to place faith in the hope that she seemed to sincerely have in me. For the life of me, I could not comprehend how I, so young, frail, and uninhibiting, could possibly inspire hope in others when, at times, I lack hope in myself. Change sits at the back of my throat; I must speak hope into existence, and then after, it shall be mine.

The wind howled a vicious hiss, and with bravery, I spoke, "Za'ara, I am ready. Should I now plant this seed?" Her demeanor once again resembled that of a child, and her spirit appeared to be uplifted. "Yes. It must take root before the storm. Here now, hurry!"

In a rushed manner, she gestured toward the brilliant porcelain pot and then tightly held on to the silver cart as to not allow the malicious wind to blow it astray. Without doubt, I placed the seed into the pocket of my left cheek, using my tongue to hold it in place, and used my hands to dig a hole in the dirt that sat in the porcelain pot. The soil was moist and rich. I spat the seed into my earthstained hand and placed it at the end of the hole, which sat at the center of the pot and, with a last look, covered it with the soil and patted it down firmly. I looked up to the glass ceiling and saw that there sat heavy gray clouds. Za'ara grabbed my arm and pulled my attention toward her. "Prepare yourself. Whatever you may hear, do not let it set fire to you. Do not allow the ill sentiments to take root in your soul. Once a seed has been planted, either hope or disease can harbor it."

I stood tall and was prepared to subject myself to the onslaught of whatever had established alarm within Za'ara. The wind blew more forcefully, and the temperature began to drop significantly more. There was a roar in the clouds, and rain began to violently fall. Rain within an enclosed room, but I did not have time to process my whereabouts nor the change in my environment. The rain fell aggressively against us, and I looked to the flowers; they strained against the heavy downpour, yet they did not bend nor break. A sharp pain shot through my ears, and my entire self was consumed with overwhelming ache. There was a loud crash, and I turned to the lovely hosts who had worn no expression, and they were not as they had been. No, instead they were on their feet in shapes of unnatural contortion, turning over the table and chairs with all their might. They were in full rage and were screaming obscenities beyond anything I had ever heard. There was no longer sadness in their eyes but only that of extreme vengeance and destruction. I could not follow the drastic change of events, and I was strongly disheartened. The handsome man with the pastel green pants was no longer handsome. He had lost all gentleness and was thrashing one of the table's fine chairs maniacally against the ground. He hissed, roared, and spat out vile proclamations of negativity and death.

"Damn this! Damn you! To hell with all that is righteous! Curse. Curses! You deserve to be lost, let the earth swallow you whole. Damn this! It's all over once you enter this vile, filthy earth. Argh! I am all that I am and all that I need!" He picked the chair up over his head and swung it unmercifully against one of the other ladies, who had previously been his amicable company.

She hit the ground and rolled over in laughter. "Ah, what a joke! What a hoot, this is fine. All is well! Hit me again! Hit me, I don't feel anything anyway. Just hit me!" She howled in laughter and spat blood on to the epoch tiling. "Merry, merry, merry! Just a good ol' time!"

I fell to my knees in horror. Just a moment ago we were sitting at a finely set table. They said nothing, they spoke not once, and now—now they only spoke words of discomfort and condemnation. I felt myself becoming sick. I could not stomach the sight of their madness; their rage was more than I could bear. The rain continued to fall; my cotton nightdress was soaked, and I was freezing cold. I yelled at the top of my voice, "Stop this! Stop!" They turned their faces to me in crooked, contorted ways and smiled. Za'ara stepped in front of me as if to protect me from them. All I understood was that this was not natural; the shift in the room's energy had drastically transformed, and it was now void of all the good that had once filled it.

"Let her play with us, beautiful Za'ara. So beautiful." The man in the pastel green pants curled his body back to his feet and stepped toward Za'ara. "Don't you miss it? Haven't you grown sick of your forsaken duties as a host? You've accomplished nothing!" He took a step back and pulled hard on his hair with closed fists. He then stepped closer now to Za'ara and was nearly a foot away from her face; with force, he screamed an anguished bellow deep from his diaphragm. He did not look at me.

He stared directly into Za'ara's eyes; she flinched not, and then she sinisterly smiled. "Yes, I do grow sick—sick of your tantrums." He lashed forward and growled maniacally, teeth snared at her face. She turned away and took a step toward me. "Hush now. I cannot do anything that you cannot do for yourself. Reason is beyond you. You are here but by your own choice." The rain was still falling; I was the only one who seemed to be uneasy in the downpour. The ladies were sitting on the ground, pulling at one another's hair and clawing at one another in a bothersome manner. They occasionally barked a spiteful comment and then rolled on the floor, cackling in response to their own demented humor.

The man in the pastel green pants stood alone in the rain; he much resembled the painting that I had seen in the grand hallway prior to entering the room. He was at the edge of the cliff; the horizon was unseen, and hope was bleak. I too sympathized with this man who had pale blue eyes, which held the sadness of all the things lost at sea. I stood with confidence and recognized his pain. No longer would I allow myself to fall to my knees at the horrors of the earth; even beauty can rise from the filth. Was I not worthy of happiness? Was he not as well? Change sat at the back of my throat, and I was fearless, a clever girl, and no such pain could rob me of my joy. Taller I stood, with purpose. The dormant potential that lived within me was useless if it slumbered for the entirety of my short life. More than anything, more than all the riches of the world, I longed to leave my mark on the hearts of others. Lifetimes could pass, and a heart could live on without ever knowing the touch of a hand who recognizes their tribulations. I am more than my hardships, and he, even in his destructive state of misery, is as well. I tilted my chin into the air and felt the rain fall upon me. Yes, beauty could rise even from the filth. I put pressure unto the heels of my feet, washing away the soil that had troubled me so against the pacifying surface of the porcelain flooring.

The storm began to die, the clouds dissipated, and silence fell upon the atrium. The heaviness that had weighed cripplingly upon my shoulders fell away, and peace found me. It sat in my heart, filled my lungs, and rested at my fingertips. I looked to the man who wore the pastel green pants; he stood there, still, with his broad shoulders slumped. The storm had nearly passed, and he would, once again, fall into silence. I stepped toward him, and Za'ara blocked me, glaring at me with stern features. I blinked my eyes and nodded my head in assurance; she understood my intention and allowed me to pass. My steps were confident, and I stood before the man; still he did not look at me.

With gentleness on my tongue I spoke, "I will not act as though I understand all that is around me. I will not pretend to know your pain or your anger. All that I know is that there is more, more than we are willing to accept, and because of it, I have hope. You too should have hope; have hope for that which sets fire to you. Do not let that fire cease to exist. If you do, then you too will cease to exist. And that would be quite a shame, would it not?"

The rain fell softly then subdued. The man lifted his head and looked at me not. The sadness had returned, sat in his eyes, and his voice was lost in the endless sea. He looked gravely at Za'ara and turned away to walk toward the other ladies. They too were now silent. They stood up off the ground and wiped their dresses down neatly. Each of them began to pick up the chairs that they had previously tossed and beaten one another with. The table was set upon its feet and was elegantly arranged with lovely cream floral peony centerpieces. Once the destruction had been organized and made to appear as though it never had happened at all, they sat at the table and poured tea. The refined tea set was of pristine quality; not one cup was shattered or made sharp. It was as it had been in the beginning. There they sat in silence, and although their faces were lovely, they wore perpetual sadness in their eyes, and their tongues knew nothing of hope. The storm of absolution had passed, and my soul's seed had been untainted.

5

———✦———

Z A'ARA BECKONED ME toward the porcelain pot
that sat unaltered on the silver cart. She harped,
"Sweet child! You are most undoubtedly a fascinat-
ing creature. Please, do tell—what did you wish to accomplish through such an ill-planned interaction?" I closed my
eyes and sighed loosely through my lips. In all honesty, I
did not act with preparation; instead, I acted upon a primal
instinct that was evoked through human compassion. I did
not believe that I acted in a manner that jeopardized my
own well-being or the well-being of Za'ara. Did she not
offer warning prior to the storms arrival? Undeniably, yes,
and by my own opinion, it was a warning well heeded. Yet I
had no answer to give to Za'ara that could properly express
the true nature of my motive.

They were forsaken, and for what reason? They fell to
curses, to the lost. Beyond comprehension, how could such
tragedy touch another? And I, for what reason other than

to evoke fear in my frail heart could I have been required to observe such atrocity. I and them, all that is happening; I felt abandoned, alone, left for naught, and the only comfort was of my own willpower, my relentless aptitude to retain such inviolable fearlessness. Yet in their eyes, though my spirit was nearly permeated by such horror, I could see that there had been defilement of basic human features in their eyes. There sat evil; there sat hate, unbelievable rage, and resentment.

So simply, I muttered, "It is enough to find ourselves alone while amongst grand company, but it is another matter completely to come to the realization that we are alone when left amongst the company of ourselves. Even more so, this place, it is not one of comfort."

Za'ara smiled again, that crooked cat smile, and laughed with full delight. "Oh, pretty darling. How you have grown so in such a short time. It is quite lovely to witness, let me assure you! Comfort is not lost in this place. True discomfort sits at the pit of your stomach; it begins to live inside of you and escapes through your pores. See, lovely dear, this is not a place of condemnation or of the unnatural. No, by all means, you have been privileged to witness the mystery of man. You should be quite excited that you have met the conditions of this room, and I, as its host, can permit you to continue forward."

A wave of relief overtook me. I had been found worthy to continue, and although I was pleased by this news, I did not particularly understand such implications. If this was not a place of condemnation, then perhaps my earlier theory of an alternate universe would stand; then I could safely assume that this anomaly was not hell at all nor purgatory. Yet how could she have such confidence in saying that this place was not one of discomfort? I was not at all in a state of comfort, nor have I been in the duration. My nightdress was still soaking wet from the passing storm. I had just witnessed man fall to madness and sorrow beyond mention, and furthermore, I spat a seed that was said to be born of my soul. None of what has happened is of common circumstance. I have been permitted to continue—permitted. And although relief overtook me, I was, at the core insulted. Who is Za'ara to grant such passage? And they, those who sat wearing such lovely faces with lasting wretchedness, did she not grant them blessing to continue? And if not, why so—what deed done could reap such consequence?

Seething resentment grew in my heart. My body trembled with rage. I extended my palms out by my side and stretched my fingers, alternating from extension to clenched fist. Faster my breath grew; heavier my sighs became. All the while I focused the matters at hand into condensing my thought process. I fed my anger and my bitterness. Heat began to rise within me. Za'ara stood where she had. She was mesmerized by the soil that cradled the said seed of my soul. Longingly she grazed the edge of the container and ran her fingers over the sculpted embellishments. With graceful hands she wafted the air above the soil, as though conjuring a spell. Still, my blood boiled.

And as I bit my tongue to keep from screaming, she scolded, "Oh, precious one. The fall is bleak. It has been drawn by no hand other than the one that steals from its own—the right from the left, the light from the dark."

She turned her right cheek to me and asked, "Have you let that which you have seen to touch your soul? For I have seen its effect." Tentatively, I approached the silver cart and peered into the soil. In it stood a small seedling at the height of no more than an inch and a quarter. It was tinted green in coloration with leaves dancing new, and atop sat a sprouting bud kissed with a flaw of gray. My spirit sank. This flaw must have stemmed from the illness that sits in my heart, the one that has hindered me my entire life. If this sapling was truly a reflection of my soul, then truly I must be as the others were: tainted. Za'ara eyed me for a moment, then tenderly she laced her arm through mine. My heart softened; the sentiments of earlier dissipated, and upon me fell realization. Tears sat in my eyes, but dare not they fall.

"How I and not the others?" With a whimper, my voice cracked. Her arm tightened, drawing me in closer. With tenderness in her voice, she responded, "Like you, they too delivered seeds of their soul, and, like you, they too underwent the storm of absolution. But unlike you, their seed did not sprout, for they were tainted long ago." She pulled my arm, as to lead me to a different direction, and together we stood before the aisles and aisles more of flowers that stood beautifully tall. She continued, "Behold all that is before you, do you not see all the beauty that has endured? While, yes, I understand that it is nearly unbearable to know that some do not bloom, you must see it as it is presented. Do you blame the seed or the hand that has harvested it? Darling, further so, do you blame the hand or the place that has harvested him? All that we are, it is by our own choosing. It is not the ocean that is angry but the wind, yet does the wind not affect the ocean so? The same is so in regards to the human soul. Were you not greatly affected by that which you witnessed? Tremendously so. To the point in which you, although in a state of unsettlement, attempted to intervene. You, lovely dear, although you are growing ever more with every passing hour, wish to evoke hope and introduce beauty to those who have already forsaken such notions. They, those who partook in the storm, have lost their voice in more than a metaphorical mean. The storm is the only period of resolve that they are granted, and such is so that they may have opportunity to speak hope, if even only for themselves."

I looked upon all that was before me. The flowers, limitless beauty; their fragrance filled the room ever so. The perfume was, if anything, enhanced by the passing storm. The gorgeous petals ebbed and flowed, swaying gracefully to the orchestral music that was playing evanescently still. By my own hand, by the strength of my own spirit, could not my soul's seed bloom and partake in the beauty that had been presented to me? I wanted nothing more than to be found worthy to join such ranks, and I had met the conditions of the room. My heart ached for those who could not move forward, but what good would I be to anyone if I was hindered by the same ailment that crippled them. I felt as though, again, I was being pulled by an unknown entity. I did not want to bid farewell to Za'ara, for I was sure that there was much more that I could earn to gain from her gentle company; but as it always is, all must move forward, and I had no doubt that forward was where I would go.

With tenderness, I placed my hand on Za'ara's and stepped away from her, looking at her strong eyes. She knew too that I intended to continue on, and sadness too sat in her eyes. "Za'ara," I whispered, "Cannot you come with me? I am unsure of what lies ahead, and I am concerned; I want to find myself back home." She smiled and fixed her hair, flattened her dress, and laughed. "Oh, sweet, sweet child. Do not allow the seed of doubt to take root in you. In all that you do, you must do it with faith. I do not have all of the answers to your questions, nor do I have the permission to continue on with you. This is now my home, but yours is elsewhere. I have faith that you will encounter all that is before you with grace and confidence." She drew her nose high into the air and was the loveliest that I had ever seen, and though I showed it not, I was comforted.

I looked once more at the sprouted seedling that fought to grow elegantly into a marvelous bloom; it was indeed the reflection of my soul, for I wanted nothing more but to flourish wonderfully in this life that I claim as my own. With farewell solemnly said, I took a step away from her and followed the calling that sat in my heart. The music played softly still, but the melody was now that of a vibrant violin solo filled with life, with hope, and it played in my mind reassuringly. I passed the table of those with lovely faces, and silently they sat, sipping their tea, noticing none but their own lonesome anguish. With my lips I sent them favor for they had none for themselves. And with that, I held on to the knob of the door, holding firmly, turning slowly. Farewell, for much had been lost and much gained.

6

━━━━━━━ ✳ ━━━━━━━

A
ND AS IT had been, my cold feet stood on the warmth of the red-and-gold Turkish rug; once again I was in the mansion hallway. Royalty would relish the lavish display of antiquity that embellished this unoccupied hall. Alone again. I wavered in the center of the hallway; the tunnel entrance that I had used previously was no longer evident. With great struggle, I pined to process all that had been. I had been in a room, a room that intended to teach a particular lesson, and the progress of the said lesson was observed by its host, the host whose origins were unknown. Her motives had seemingly been of true nature, yet unnaturally so, not all of that which was demonstrated was of sound understanding. I had met the conditions of that room by no means but of my own. Yes, such was of my own doing, but I dared not allow confidence to be manipulated to pride, for pride is a fool's faulty weapon. I steadied myself. Za'ara had spoken of others

who were many times successful, success in terms of the fall of others. It was quite essential to be speculative of all, to maintain constant awareness; my steps must continue crucially confident.

Forward now, forward always. The sounds of the atrium were left behind, the lessons not. There was no change in the setting of the hall; all was wonderfully designed. Two, four, six. Two, four, six. I became uneasy. I stepped confidently nonetheless, with grace, but the still small voice within spoke warning. To it, I heeded. Words of hope sat on my tongue and consoled me, for the only downfall that could make me prey would be of my own doubt. The lighting in the hall became faint; the air was unexpectedly polluted with dank cigarette smoke. The exhalation of a smoker's lung hung heavy and heavier more as I journeyed farther into the hallway. The walls became bare; no longer was there the tone that had been previously set in design. The smoke stung my eyes, and they became dry; I squinted to focus my hazy vision. The walls seemed dilapidated, to gradually alter from the extravagant cream walls that had previously furnished the fine corridor. I made sure to stay in the center of the walkway; the smell had become more unbearable, and I put my hand over my mouth. Soot sat on the carpet, small bits here, portions there, and then more.

I placed my hand on the wall, it truly was changing, yet such manipulation, I could not identify the hand that caused this shift. The touch beneath my fingertips was of a different texture; I put pressure on my fingers and felt that the wall was now of solid rock—gray, dark, cut into sharpness, like that of natural stone that laid jagged on a mountain's side. With caution, I approached the wall and placed a soft hand upon it; it was damp and cold. Looking to my right, I saw the continuation of the hall. There seemed to be quite some way to walk, but the lighting did not permit me to see past the length of my own arm. I kept my hand on the stone and walked farther on, proceeding cautiously of my every step, ensuring that I placed appropriately the heel of my foot to its palm. Watchfully, I forged ahead, urging my eyes to focus in the fading light. Then, with another step, my foot found moisture, and then my other foot did as well. The carpeting was now wet with water—perhaps heavy condensation from the stone? I attempted at another breath for air, but it was still filthy with cigarette smoke. I stepped along some considerable steps more, keeping my left hand on the stone wall and my right over my nose and mouth.

Then, when squinting very tightly and focusing ten times more, I was able to see what vaguely appeared to be the lining of an entrance to a cave. I had been told not to allow that which I saw to have great affect over me, and having been exposed to strange events beforehand, the sight did not utterly astonish me. I swallowed hard and continued to my newfound destination. I recalled all that had happened; many more were waiting, many who had been many times successful. Although I knew not what I was preparing for, I was preparing all the same. My mind leapt from the logical to the illogical; it attempted to process that which it could not understand. Who awaited me in the darkness of the cavern? What otherworldly condition was to be met; and, even more, would I be allowed to continue forward? Many others were before me, and many times they were successful. If I were to fail, would I become as those with the lovely faces? Unendingly voiceless, burdened by everlasting sadness. I could not allow such to become of myself. And as I treaded in the dampened soot, before me was the unsettling, gaping entrance of the stone cave. It was consumed by absolute darkness; the focus of vision that I had found was now lost. Apprehension ran rabid at the forefront of my willingness to subject myself, the flames of purpose rose wildly within me, and, with confident steps, I entered the stone cavern.

As I walked through the mouth of the cave, it was evident that it was the source of the strong smell of cigarette; the smell offended me. The transition of a room filled with the wonderful aroma of perfumed flowers to that of the ashes that fell from burned tobacco churned my stomach. I stood in what looked to be the largest space in the cavern, it was circular in form; the floor was no longer damp, and humidity hung heavily in the air. I looked to my wrists to see if, by chance, I had an elastic hair band, but chance did not favor me. My brown hair, which usually sat straight, was not in a sightly condition whatsoever. From pouring rain to thick humidity, I was not a sight to behold. My attention was quickly pulled from myself by a light that danced compellingly against the stone walls, and what sat around me was nothing I could have foreseen.

The source of light was provided by that of a child's toy, half sphere in shape. From it a soothing lullaby played, and as it revolved, it projected shapes and shadows upon the walls. The shadows were composed of figures, and as they danced horribly upon the walls, I could see the details of this stone room. The room was that of a child's nursery. Against the room's edge was a wooden crib that sat empty and childless. In the crib laid archaic, white tattered bedding that time and neglect had yellowed—not suitable for a child at all. Near it was a worn bookcase, with books of assorted types tossed unsympathetically unto its shelves and the surrounding floor. And beyond, was that of a sight quite peculiar. On the walls were lace white curtains arranged and tied in a homely display, but behind them there was no window.

My heart sank; my awareness elevated. How undeniably dismal. To be shut into a room with no light yet to accommodate so in the event that such may arrive as though the curtains were an invitation, a demonstration of hope. However, in a place such as this, perhaps at a time in the past, there had indeed sat windows. Perhaps at one time, the curtains did in fact serve a purpose, but now, that purpose was no longer evident. The half sphere continued to spin, casting both small and large shadows, and they danced. Not the sweet dance of a ballerina, no. The music was that of a lovely ballet sung by tiny mechanical sprockets and springs, but the shadows danced without grace and not at all with rhythm. The figures moved as though pulled by strings, like puppets at the hand of a puppeteer. They were merely shadows, shadows all the same. They did not have faces, no expressions, and no life, yet if I could name one for them, why, I would not. Because it would all be too terribly bleak in nature.

Then there was a creak. A creak from near the curtained wall. The color fell from my face, and a short gasp escaped my lips. Swiftly, I turned, and though I wished awfully hard that I would not need to open my eyes and see what was there, I convinced myself that I must. Two, four, six. And there was nothing. Nothing but an old, tired rocking chair with a flattened cushion that gathered dust. Great relief filled me, and I disconcertingly rearranged my disheveled nightdress. How silly of me to overreact and entertain the fear that crept on me. Of the many things I was not, one thing I undoubtedly was, was fearless. Yes, I must remember that which makes me myself. I tilted my chin up and teased my hair. I turned in the direction that the half sphere rotated in, following its cast of light. And as I stepped along, walking in a large round circle at the steady pace of the light, on the stone wall was writing carved into them. A poem inscribed in the dark stone. I paced closer, with light feet, forcing my eyes to focus and as the sphere went round slowly, I spoke aloud the words that the light permitted:

"Hush. Silence shall shroud you, sweet child. Fear not the moon, she wishes only to bestow soft kisses unto your splendid cheek. Cry not, fearful one—do you recognize those that sit in the shadowed night? They stalk only to steal your bliss; sleep soundly, precious darling, do not permit the dark ones to delight."

My lips hung parted, and my fingers raised to shut them close. This poem, the inscription, did it speak of the darkness that sat and mockingly observed me throughout my entire—no, such could not possibly be. Panic settled in my heart, and I began to feel anxious. What is this? An attack against my most personal fears? Yet I had never breathed a single word expressing such fears. No, it only sat in my heart, it was mine alone, but how could such be written. That which I had read had struck a personal chord, a chord that I preferred not be plucked. I stared at the carved inscription with wide eyes, and then, quickly, with my peripheral vision, I saw a shadow that danced faster than the others.

Again, I turned in a sudden motion to catch that which lurked behind me. Now, in the dust covered rocking chair, sat a shadowed figure of a man, and on his face he wore a sharpened smile.

My hand sat on my mouth, and there were no words ready to be said. The shadowed man leaned back in the chair and crossed his right leg over his left, rocking the chair backward. In his hand was a lit cigarette, but he did not hold it to his mouth. I was frozen; this figure, the energy he emitted—he was not to be trusted, he posed threat. I straightened my spine and took a step calmly back. With a high-pitched howl, he roared in laughter; kicking back his rocker with greater force. His hand flicked the cigarette butt to the ground. He leaned forward, placing both his hands forcefully against the arms of the rocker and inclined hastily forward, and at that he smiled. His smile was of a mouth of sharpened teeth, corroded with disease and all things foul. I despised this shadowed man. He was not even truly a man at all.

He stood no taller than four feet in height and was one and a half in width. His legs were not even in length, a small lopsided eyesore he was! He lunged off the rocker, and with his hobbled leg, twisted his foot over the cigarette butt. Of the many terrible things I knew he was capable of, he hunched toward me, still wearing that stained smile. Two, four, six. I kept my breaths even; I could not permit him to detect my fear, to read my troubled body language. To no avail. He squirmed and wriggled his body in devilish delight.

"Are you truly fearless, little miss? Or is it that your pearly conscious has you convinced?" He spoke in a high-pitched snarl; the sound irked my ear and filled me with disgust. Pig. He took another step toward me and then hobbled in a larger circle around me.

"I pray it is the darkness that you cannot resist." He lurched slowly around me, observing me, clearing his throat of phlegm, and coughing it on to the floor. He'd laugh. He would look at me and cackle, throwing his head back and releasing a demeaning squeal. My chin stayed scornfully in the air; not an inch of my being desired to acknowledge his imp presence. He mocked me; this I knew, and such was his wicked intention. He tempted my spirit toward anger. My nostrils flared, but I must not let him irk me; to answer his bothersome antics with harshness would be to recognize his intention. I will not entertain him. I thought of Za'ara, how she had handled herself with poise. I had learned much from her, and to this shadow, I would demonstrate all that she had instilled in me.

The shadowed man still circled me, but I did not let him cause intimidation. Light shone around the room, still by the half sphere. Other shadow figures and shapes danced on the wall, but in them was no animation. I tilted my head

back and stretched it to both sides, encouraging composure and confidence. I turned to the ill-willed shadow and
sternly glared at him. He smiled crookedly. I faced my body
toward that of his and then proceeded to sit cross-legged
on the cold ground. He watched as I settled my body comfortably on the floor, and I flashed a cocky smile at him.

"I thought that, perhaps, if I sat down, you would feel
somewhat more intimidating. That is your intention, is it
not? To evoke fear in me." I was rather proud of myself;
however, I could not prevent the terrible tremble in my
voice. Although I acted in fearlessness, in resilience towards
his inapt demeanor, I could not disregard the sickening
sentiment that sat in my stomach. I kept my eyes on his
face, but his face could not be depicted. He was a shadow, a
figure of a contorted man. His only defining characteristic
was that of his vile smile, which he had never let drop. I
sighed heavily and prepared myself for what was ahead; I
worried that I would not be as easily able to move forward
from this dark, stone cavern.

The imp had continued walking in his circle, heaving
his body up and down to walk as efficiently as he could. I
heard his steps stop when he was standing directly behind
me. I stiffened. "I see, I see. An exceptional child I heard
you would be. I worry not, for both you and me, we know
that you suffer greatly from a particular disease." Anxiety
stunned my senses. I looked to the wall that wore the poetic

inscription. All was true. See, I am of a stubborn sort, and to admit my faults is to give them life. I was undoubtedly fearless, but what provoked me most of all was that I doubted my ability to fear less. I am ravaged by doubt, by fear, and it has always been the human condition that has caused me great unease. Often I would find myself doubting all that I had come to accept. I had accepted that I was fearless, but here, in this abandoned child's nursery set in stone, I could not abstain from the fall into fear. Doubt was the disease that I suffered heavily from, the ailment that riddled me useless year upon year. The cause of the gray flaw that kissed the blooming bud of my soul's seed. How could I, so small, so profoundly unworthy, be capable of touching the hearts of others, to be the root of inspiration? I sat cross-legged on the ground in near darkness, haunted by a shadow that saw all of my most reserved intricacies—the secrets that I had held so closely to my hardened heart.

7

———— ⚹ ————

I T WAS QUITE liberating to admit such fault after having been in denial for so very long. Time was not to
be spent in celebration though, no. I had to face the
self-rectification that I was to mentally and emotionally
undergo. I had come to acknowledge the fear that resided
within me; it was time now, to acknowledge that which I
feared, that which stood unnervingly behind me. I placed
both hands alongside my crossed legs and turned my body
around and positioned myself so that I would be facing the
shadowed figure. I then laid my legs against one another to
the side of me. I faced the manifested fear that was before
me and spoke quietly. "I know not what you are, or how you
have come to be, but I know who I am and likewise how
I have come to be such. You speak of this great disease; I
know it all too well. I have endured it, battled with it. I am
the fearful one, the one whose lullaby is inscribed on the
stone wall. This I understand because it is what I have come

to terms with, but what I do not understand is how you have come to know of it. Tell me now, I must know."

I sat, staring sternly at this entity, and he growled in amusement. His body swelled in delight, and his animal smile widened across his absent face. He took two or so steps back and placed his hand on the arm of the rocking chair. He turned to me and gaped his horrid mouth in further laughter. He mocked me still, even after my demonstration of self-awareness. I grit my teeth to hold the obscenities that fought to free themselves from my livid mouth. I placed my hands calmly unto my lap, exasperatingly yet patiently awaiting his vile response. Two, four, six.

He twisted his body back into the dusty rocker and kicked himself back with spirit on his heel. After he found himself in a quite comfortable position, he placed his head on his elbow and continued to laugh horridly. It took every ounce of patience to sit motionless and be ridiculed by this atrocity. I tucked my tongue into the side of my cheek and endured his tasteless humor. After what seemed to be ages, he halted his rocker and sat attentively, proclaiming this, "Do you know why I laugh on your behalf? Because you are a liar! A liar beseeching truth. The truth! So young, naive, until you come clean, you will receive no answers from me!" He roared violently, cackling in laughter at a matter that was not at all amusing. I despised him all the more; my tongue could not be kept from lashing.

"How dare you, you abhorrent creature!" I spit out in rage and slammed my hand against the stone ground in protest. My eyes glared at him wildly; I hissed out breaths of air, and my blood burned. The shadows cast by the half sphere projector continued to dance on the wall. The lullaby played, sweetly so; the tranquility that they represented angered me further. I did not want to be in this place anymore. Cigarette smoke still hung in the air, but now that I sat here furiously on the ground, I could see that there was so much more to this room. The ceiling was low, the temperature high. Sweat beaded my brow; how had I not noticed the intense heat before? Perhaps I had fussed myself into a fever. I looked around the room more, trying to calm myself. This figure, he spoke in rhymes and tested my patience. I placed both hands on the ground and lifted myself to my feet. I must compose myself. This is what he wanted; he does not deserve the reward of another success.

The shadows danced at the edge of the nearing light; these solitary souls lingered in shameful secrecy. I was uncertain if this beaten path would lead me astray; sometimes I wondered if this unknown place would incinerate every reminisce of hope. I walked closer to where the crib sat and looked at the figures that danced on the wall. They were of shapes and figures, not horrible nor pleasant. They simply were. Careless, devoid of life, dancing casually with no worry. Yes, perhaps they were merely shadows projected by a child's plaything, simply the manipulation of light, but there had been a time when I was just the same. Merely existing, alive without life, living amongst the extraordinary yet posing no question or criticism. Laughter escaped me—a small giggle—and I turned to the shadowed creature.

"Perhaps maybe I do understand why you laugh insatiably. You take delight in the art of deception; and might I say that you are truly indeed an artist. You nearly captured me. Truly, you are quite resourceful, testing your ingenuity on the weak of heart!" I walked toward the bookcase that was haphazardly displayed and began to pick up the books, placing them neatly on the shelves. While doing so, I continued to speak in a demeaning tone of voice toward the shadow. "In all honesty, I searched my mind for the reasons that you felt the authority to speak so brazenly to me. It was quite rude to call me a liar, especially when the case is that you are and I at all."

The shadowed figure flashed a fascinated smile and sat forward in his seat. His sneer spread ear to ear, and he jeered, "Now this is fun, such fun, yes! It has been quite a while since I have met an individual this worthwhile. And now, if I have your permission, pretentious miss, can I ask why you dismiss yourself as a liar and throw me instead into the fire?" He thoroughly enjoyed this playtime, seeing as that was all he considered this to be. I had been right in discerning his lack of trustworthiness. I walked about the room displaying confidence, but truth be told, I walked only to keep myself from trembling. I wished this creature to death. It was him who I wished would fall to silence like those that I had seen before. To stay in motion was merely to keep myself aware of my actions, of myself.

With a dry tongue, I retorted, "You speak in rhyme, and you sit in a child's nursery. Though it lacks the delight of one, it has fallen to shambles, quite literally. The words that are carved into the stone—that is how you know my weaknesses. See, I have come to understand that this is a place of the unnatural; so if my mindset is that of the natural, I would most surely fall victim to your game. I have been taught better though. How it has come to be, I have no answer, but I believe that those who find themselves lost in this room's darkness, their inner turmoil comes to be displayed on the wall in the form of a poem. That is the only reason you know where my ailments sit, not of your own knowledge or observation but only because it has been set before you so conveniently."

I swallowed hard; doubt sat in my throat, but I did not choke. I continued, "I rather enjoy games as well. As a child, I would sit and play often, sometimes alone, sometimes not, but because of my cleverness, I always was victorious even in the most minimalistic ways. Perhaps you are not a liar but only a partial liar, seeing as you only told a partial truth. This is the reason I became so irate when you spat out such a rude comment, such as naming me a liar, it truly did hurt but not for the reason you think. It only bothered me so because, in this case—in this one great experience—this is truly the most honest I have ever been. So you bruised my pride, an attribute that I have been working tirelessly to abandon. And as for your earlier comment, I have come clean. I confess that I am fearful, that doubt does at times plague me; I might be somewhat pretentious, somewhat removed, but I too have observed many things, and that which I take most delight in is the ability to acknowledge my faults and mend them before I fall prey to the many that are much like you."

I basked in the lovely warmth of the self-honor that filled me. Za'ara had been a host that wanted only to lead me to the truth, and this shadow host, much unlike Za'ara, wished to lead me to further confusion. And all that I had said had been the absolute truth. I did believe myself to be clever, and though I admitted some few strengths, I also did note many faults as well. A liar would not be capable of doing so; to be a liar is to be a master of manipulation, and to master such art, you must first be manipulated by your own hand. I believed that I knew how to leave this foul room—how to free myself of this parasite host. He had not spoken a word since I had stopped speaking, not even another patronizing chuckle. Perhaps he assumed that I would continue, or perhaps he would not speak until I stumbled and he found fault or inaccuracy in that which I said. Ah, yes! That must be it. He could only feed off the faults that I strongly displayed, but if I demonstrated them not, then how could he speak any longer? He would have no other option but to grant me passage from this life-stealing room.

I had much spirit but took caution in how I would approach such subject matter. I swept my hair to one side and began to braid it, knowing that it would only fall loose again. I whispered hope internally and thought of my sapling that sat on the silver cart in the room past. I wished only that it would grow strong and encourage others to find their voice. With that in mind, I changed my inner mindset. I breathed deeply in through my nose and exhaled with my mouth, and with softness, I directed a question to the shadow man who sat expectantly on the rocker. "I now I have a question for you, if you'd be so generous as to entertain me. How long have you been in this room?"

He smiled gravely and adjusted himself in his seat. "Why, I never have quite thought of putting a time stamp on the duration that I've sat here in this room. If I must be generous, then I will say for all time, if I do presume."

He nearly confirmed my theory. "Why, all time is a long time," I whispered. I came to the wall with the inscription on it and sat, speaking again, "Do you see the dancing figures on the wall?"

And to that he answered, "Yes, they too have been there for all time and time more."

I smirked and asked again, "And we have agreed that a long time is time enough, have we not?"

He turned his absent face to the side, rested it on his hand, and agreed, "Well, yes, a long time is a long time, Miss. What is your question? You are beginning to fuss, and it is very irritating, I've nearly had quite enough." I began to crawl to the center of the room, to where the half sphere sat, and I reached out to it, and the shadowed man yelled ferociously, "Do not touch that! Do not touch that. It has been there always, do not touch what is not yours."

I pulled my hand back and spoke, "That is true. It is not mine, but neither is it yours."

He gasped and growled, jumping off the rocking chair and hobbled toward me. He shrieked louder yet, saying "I have more right to it than you do!"

I stood up, holding the half sphere. The light continued to project, but the images now were being cast all around the room, from the ground to the ceiling, to behind the curtains where no window sat at all.

The shadowed man was ravaged with fury, yet he did not demonstrate any particular strength at all. "You see, shadowed sir, look behind me. I have what you are." Behind me was my own shadow. A figure of myself in the blackest black, that followed me always, observing all that I did.

"See? The reason that it has life is because I cast my own upon it. You, sir, do not have life but are simply a trick of the light. This is what I think. You have stolen the shadows of the others who have been here. They are captured in this half sphere; you are also a collector, a collector of things that do not belong to you. You hold them here as puppets that you can watch dance on the walls for your own pleasure for all time, stealing the life force that was given freely to them for your own gain. And you have the audacity to call me a liar. Well, shadowed sir. You have now lost."

With that said, I raised the half sphere above my head and threw it strongly against the ground, shattering it to many little pieces. He bellowed out in great agony. Many shadows escaped from the half sphere and flew chaotically along the rooms edges, with great speed like that of a colony of bats; then, in an ecstasy of newfound freedom, they danced out of the large mouth of the cave. The yelling had stopped, and as I turned to see where the shadowed man had gone, he was nowhere to be seen. I looked around the room for traces of what he had been. I looked to the curtains that hung on the wall, and between them now was a portrait of a shining sun, and on the green earth that it shone so brightly on was the shadow of a hobbled man that lay upon its green grasses. He did not look as though he was glad to be there—no, not at all; it was as though the sun burned him greatly, causing him great pain. I looked to the corner of the portrait, and a named was signed: Maelzer. Maelzer—that is what I shall call the shadowed man, the man who was no more than a trick of the light, a great manipulator, a liar, and a deceiver.

And with that, I turned to walk out from the room's great darkness, for my lungs still had not accepted the terrible smell of cigarette. I suppose that I had met this room's condition and was then, therefore, allowed to move forward from this dreary place. I stepped carefully around the broken pieces of glass that had been of the half sphere and looked at the wall that had had the poetic inscription. My eyes adjusted to see once more, but it was no longer as it had been. Now it sat with letters etched in gold, and it shone quite beautifully in contrast to the darkness of the room. It warned, "Be weary, courageous one, for many will envy that which sits in your brave heart. Your spirit is stubborn to protect that which is right, but in all that you do, know that your purpose must be first in your passionate sight. The fire sits at your left, urging you boldly, but brashly you will be cast into further darkness. The fire, which is ready to aid, is also quick to devour you if you are to be found, at all, afraid."

I swallowed hard and memorized what had been written. Another warning. I blinked hard and began to walk slowly out of the mouth of the cave. I kept watch for the shadows that had bolted from the cave, but none were to be seen. I saw the tunnel's end but did not continue to walk. I stopped and began to quietly weep. How I had kept so much weighing profoundly upon me for so long, for all of time; and now, when liberation seemed to be within reach, I come to find that such would not be so easily. I cried serenely into my hands when finally I understood what I believed this place to be. How much more would I need to endure before I could be home again? And why, after so many years of incredible agony, had I now only begun to have such a great epiphany?

This must be punishment for all that I had represented in the past. I had been a girl who had done what she must and not more. This shadowed man, Maelzer, he taunted my past self. She had been one who would lay in bed awake for all hours of the day. She was a manipulator, a liar, not only of others, but of herself. I had been convinced that was all that there was, that life was simply to be endured and that the many would remain particularly unawarded. How foolish I had been. Za'ara had told me that I had come to grow so quickly, but Maelzer only sung of how quickly I could relapse and fall back into the habits that had been burdensome to me before. Bravely I wiped the tender tears away from my eyes, leaving them on the hem of my night-dress sleeve. No longer would I simply endure the anguish that had been incessantly cast upon me; I would simply not accept them as my own any longer.

And with that, I steadied myself. More now than ever was I prepared to further subject myself to this place of the unnatural. This place where the impossible was simply that of the possible—unlimited. I knew not what lay before me, but with purpose and passion, I would embrace them and conquer them all. I was standing at the mouth of the cave, upon the edge of the grand Turkish rug that was somewhat still dampened. I walked further and saw that nothing had changed, yet I knew that soon now, I would be led by that which had brought me already to places beyond that of the comprehendible.

8

———— ❋ ————

I PAUSED AT the foot of the elaborate carpet and looked suspiciously around at the calm surroundings of the solitary hallway. I did not know where I was to go next. I was more than sure that there would be a palpable change, a sign that would lead me in the direction that I must go next, but there was not. All was as it had been. I walked on into the hallway. My heart was encouraged; it had been necessary that I recognized all that must be released, for it had only held me from all that I was sure to become. I wondered if the door that led back to Za'ara was still there. I had so many more questions and was becoming quite disoriented to everything that had taken place in what seemed to be during such a short span of time. I shut my eyes, isolating my sense of hearing, but heard nothing at all; no one was calling me. I was sure that I would be called upon, though; no worry sat in my heart. Though I was eager to experience more, I used this unoc-

cupied time as an opportunity to venture this place that I
had no name for.

I felt abrupt joy in my heart—unadulterated joy—and I
could not resist the urge to move. My feet were light, and
my face wore a smile of sincerity; and I danced. A step
forward, then back, and then to the side—a graceful twirl.
My spirit overflowed with joy, and I simply danced and
laughed sweetly, glad to be in the company of myself. Truly
I felt a great happiness that I have never had had the pleasure of experiencing before. To describe this joy, let me see:
It was as though peace had finally found me after all this
time. I had come to accept that peace did not privilege the
doubtful, and such explained the reason for its absence in
my life for so long. For once I undressed myself of restless-
ness; I found myself worthy of receiving such a wonderful gift, the gift of internal rest. As I danced, I let loose
every doubt, inhibition, every past stumble, and breathed
life anew. Now, more than any time before, I wholeheartedly knew what I wished to represent more than anything
in all of the world. I twirled twice more then came to a stop.
There was a mirror. It sat tall and broad, covering the hall
from each corner of the ceiling to each corner of the floor.
Looking into it, I could see that the mouth of the cave did
not sit behind me any longer. I turned to study what it had
become instead, and now, it was simply just the ending of a
commonplace hall.

I stood staring at the mirror, and the reflection of myself stared assuredly back. I approached the mirrored wall with calm steps and a tilted head. I did not walk that of a straight line, not at all; I wanted to test the spirit that was reflected to me, and the test she impressively failed. A reflection is no more than merely an image of what is being presented to it, but this spirit, she did not mirror the movements that I made. She stood straight at the center of the mirror with her arms at her side. Her hair was the same, her lips, eyes, and face, but she had something additional. I could not understand how I could look at an image of myself in the mirror and know that it was not I at all. She did not move nor speak; not a blink was made. With a furrowed brow and a perplexed demeanor, I approached the reflection until I was no more than a foot away.

I imitated her posture. She was I, but the language that her body resonated was with so much more poise than that of my own. I brushed the loose hair from my face then rolled back my shoulders and straightened my spine, adjusting myself to elegantly display proper posture as well. For a moment, we simply stared at one another. I would cock my head at a certain angle, and similarly would she. Wrapping my arms around one another, I held myself and shuddered. How absolutely eerie. Goosebumps covered my skin, leaving trails from my neck to my frozen fingertips. It is absolutely one phenomenon to look in the mirror and see a reflection of yourself, but it is another matter altogether to know that that reflection is likewise regarding you tentatively in return as well.

I casually extended one arm toward the mirror and placed my fingertips against its incandescent surface. With little effort, I applied minimal force. And just very briefly, I was disappointed. For no reason at all, except by that of my own imagination, I assumed that perhaps the mirror would act as a doorway, but it did not. I had been taught to assume beyond that of the natural; with more force, I pushed my palm intensely harder unto the surface but, again, to no avail. I was unreasonably thwarted. I looked at the reflection of myself in the mirror to find her looking at me with compassionate brown eyes. As my hand sat against the surface, she reached her hand forward to meet it. There we were, in that one fleeting moment, unquestionably united. Her hand touched my own on the mirror, and an electric shock traveled through my body, I was left breathless. Colors, memories, and flashes of then and now all relentlessly raced across my mind, and somehow I was able to process the limitless revelation that was being exposed to me. All that had been in the comfort of my home and in all that I had endured in this place as well—then, nothing at all. I blinked rapidly then opened my eyes in astonishment; I immediately removed my hand from hers. She smiled warmly and kindly inquired, "Do you understand now?"

I did. She took a step to the side and asked again, "Do you? You must. If I do, then you must also." I stepped in the opposite direction that she did.

With an eager tongue I urged, "I do, but how? You are merely a reflection of myself as displayed by this mirror. Are you trapped? Let me free you!"

She laughed as jovially as I had before when dancing lightheartedly in the hall just not too long ago. "I have no worries that you will! It is just a matter of time and doubly so a matter of willingness. Neither are troubles that will set you back though, at least not in great distances. Isn't such news exciting? I am so glad to finally know that you know me. It has taken our entire life to orchestrate such an engagement!" She spoke with such illicit excitement, with uninterrupted enthusiasm. Never had I had such great comfort nor a grander sign of hope for that which was to come. I looked at the mirror and saw not myself but the promise of what I was intended to be.

This young woman in the mirror—it was no question that she and I were alike but not at all the same. Again, the supernatural aspects of this universe baffled me unequivocally. When we met at the mirror and touched, it was as though we had connected on a level beyond that of emotion or physicality. She shared with me visions. I know not how to explain it, not even in the sense that would appease that of even my own mind, but in the simplest of terms, this I could say and it would stand true: The woman in the mirror, she had been me, and I was to become her. I supposed that this ideology was most unrealistic; when the visions had passed in my mind, I saw memories that I had experienced, but I also saw circumstances that had not come to pass as well. Yet all the while, in my mind I could hear her voice speak truth unto me. Furthermore, as improbable as it may seem to be, I believed that she was the version of myself that I so longed to become.

I held my hand to my chest in astounding disbelief. It was so very amazing; I had just wished to have the answers to my many questions and had hoped to find Za'ara in the atrium once more, but that was not what was meant at this point in time. I had to get the answers from myself in an unbelievably literal sense. My alter persona was awaiting my response patiently on the other side of the mirror. On the other side, I knew it was a place similar to this one. One of supernatural happenings, one of absolute clarity. From what I was shown, I would arrive there in the future when I was more prepared. With my every day, I would work ever so diligently every day until I do. The wonderful joy had returned to my heart, and I was pleased. I turned excitedly to the mirror and spoke to myself, to the reflection that not only showed me my future self but also allowed me to interact with her as well. I had immense faith that I would become all that she represented; I was a willing vessel.

I still had many questions, though, and to her, I inquired, "Is it all right if I call you Fé? It would be strange to call you by my own name, although it is your name as well."

She smiled and laughed; she did this much more often than I did. She wiped underneath her eye and cheerfully responded, "I like it very much, and it suits me quite well actually. All right, now that that is settled, we can discuss the matter at hand. It is so important that you take everything that I share with you to heart." Her demeanor changed, and it demonstrated sternness. With a tight lip, she continued, "How are you handling everything thus far? Have you come to understand what it all represents? What its primary purpose is?"

I sighed. Za'ara had asked the same questions. Maelzer had provoked the same as well. I had not come to a grand conclusion. No ultimate revelation had dawned upon me, and still, I was learning from these precise experiences that provoked certain personal qualities that had been dormant in me for quite some time. I did not need to have an answer; I could speak with Fé, and surely she would assist in the organization of my frame of mind. She would guide me. "Fé, it has been difficult to understand everything around me, I've been able to digest portions of it, but I do not have an absolute answer."

"I see," she whispered, bowing her head. "Then tell me what you do know, you must know something beyond that of a doubt."

Truth be told, I did not want to seem erratic. None of that which I could say would calm that of a sound mind; it was beyond imagination. Speaking unpleasantly would cause me great discomfort; if there was a slip from my tongue, my tongue could so very easily paint me as mad. She still stood there with her head bowed, as though I had dissatisfied her. Yes, I understood what she had shown me, but how could everything be true? I looked away. I could not bear to be a disappointment. I could not face the reflection of my alternate self questioning my thoughts and my intentions. It could not be tolerated. The joy had been stolen from me by the hand of her who stood as a mirrored image, representing that which I was being led to become. How unworthy to be unable to confront even myself.

The taste in my mouth was dry. Frustration saturated my demeanor, I felt small. Again, after having felt so wonderfully—to be belittled by the reality of my own shortcomings. I despised my inability to nurture inspiration in spans no longer than that of a moment of excitement. This has always been a detrimental aspect of my personality. Inspiration came in bursts, but my desire dwindled as quickly as it had come. Such is my fatal flaw; to live life truly, must you not be invested, encouraged? Doubt is venomous;

it steals, kills, and destroys. Furthermore, it succeeds. Worse of all, I did not wander in the unknown, no. I, more than anyone, understood that that which sets your soul on fire, that which gives you purpose—it must be adamantly pursued. Here I was in this place; each encounter tested both my weaknesses and strengths. Each individually imperative to the contents of my character, each which made me uniquely able to do that which I believe I was called to do. I was being prepared, yet, as quickly as the inspiration to urge myself forward came, it also left. This was not of my own doing. It had been the doing of life itself.

So very often I used this as an excuse. Life—a dead reason to feel at ease in the skin that was increasingly constricting me, continuously choking me. I was bound to the physical by that which made me man, but evermore I craved meaning for more than the eye could capture. More. It was what I passionately wanted: more truth, more depth, more understanding, more purpose. It is quite ironic, though, that which I used as protection was in fact the cause of my undying distress. Sudden pangs of anxiety would seize the surface of my skin; scattered goosebumps would freckle the superficial. I was my own downfall, my own poison. Life did not bring such burden to me; I brought it upon myself. Doubt did not force itself upon me; I simply accepted it. Fear did not steal from me; I selfishly stole from myself. Here I was in this place of reconciliation, and even here did I run from that which was so obvious. I dared not allow my own tongue to curl and form the words that I could not accept. How could I admit such reality to another when I had yet to accept it for myself? My lips were kept tightly shut, and I was left silently screaming, burning in the fire of my own self-contempt. The fire, how it had dwindled unremittingly in my spirit. But stubbornly, just as I, it refused to be ignored.

Fé still stood there silently, but her head was not bowed. She faced me sternly, and visible anger sat on her face. We were connected beyond that of this interaction, beyond that of this mirrored wall. She represented the self that I had denied. She had reason to be angry, to be cross with me. See, in the vision that she shared with me, it was a glimpse into the time that was promised to come—the future. She is the future, and I am the past. Her valid reason to hold irritation against me, well, it was more than understandable. If I cannot—if I am still unable to—overcome all that is being set before me, then she, Fé, this vision of my future self, would never come to exist and I, only I, would be the sole bearer of such fault.

With shame I drew my eyes up to meet hers, and when they did, I turned around, giving her my back. I could not face her; I was not able to carry such responsibility. "Will you not fight against the crippling self-doubt? You are worthy. I am too. Talk to me; speak what's on your heart. Please, or all that you have seen, it will never come to be."

She spoke with unwaning fear. I lifted my chin, turning my cheek to her. With almost no voice at all, I muttered, "You are an image of my future self, the self that I should strive to become. Tell me how I can overcome all that debilitates me. I will follow, but alone, I am lost, and while lost, I can accomplish very little." She too turned around. Our backs faced one another, separated by a mirror in the hallway, decorated in golds and reds. I felt our connection slowly fading away into near nothingness. Then, very faintly, I heard the sound of the sad violin solo playing lamentingly through the paper walls.

With boundless willingness, I turned around and confessed with immense pain in my voice, "I am unworthy, so greatly am I unworthy, but all the others—my family, my friends, even the strangers whose sad eyes I meet in streets—they are. I understand what I am to do, the amount of sacrifice that is needed to accomplish all that I recognize as my indisputable purpose. I am just a girl, so human, and that which is meant for me is so extraordinary. Why is becoming who I am meant to be so very difficult, and why must I learn in this strange way?" There was no sadness in my voice, only that of frustration and impatience.

She circled back and stared at me; there was no demonstrated expression, and then she spoke, "Is that what holds you back? That you will need to sacrifice many things in your life?"

Yes, and I knew that that seemed very selfish of me for many reasons—for the reason that if I continued this way, she would not come to exist. Or even more selfishly so, that I would not be permitting myself to move forward, forever condemning myself to the lifestyle of a witness who sees but takes no action.

I understood, yet there was more, so I spoke with little hesitation and muttered back, "Do not think of me in that light, that is not the light that I wish to project. It is simply this, if not anything else; to be of the world, there are certain commonalities that have been deemed as normality. This has been decided by the many, the majority. They are strong, perhaps not emotionally because their emotions they keep captive in their ribcages, but this, this that is being asked of me would thrust me into the minority." I held my breath. My tongue had forsaken me; it had left me vulnerable, and I waited for the reaction that it had caused.

Fé stood, eyes squinted, mouth hung open slightly; she had no words. She closed her eyes and smiled. "Do you hear that?"

I turned around, faced her, and said, "Yes."

Her eyes remained closed, and she inhaled a deep breath. "The violin. We played as children, though not as well as we could have." Her laugher escaped her mouth in a small puff. There were soft creases around her eyes when she smiled;

it softened my heart. "If you concentrate, you can smell the faint perfumes of the lovely flowers that I know you admire so very much."

I submitted and, with a deep breath, allowed their wonderful smell to calm me.

"Do you not remember the lesson that you learned when in the atrium?"

I knew that she proceeded to prove a point; I did not fight her. "Of course I remember. Za'ara is a teacher that I could never forget."

"It is not only that. She was not the lesson that you needed to learn. She was merely a messenger. What was the message that she taught you?"

I thought back to the room filled with the lovely flowers, I recalled all that I had seen. "She wanted to teach me hope. That without hope, there can be no beauty. That beauty without hope is empty and, ultimately, is not beautiful at all."

"And what else?"

"What else?"

"Yes. You understood the concept that you were intended to, which is wonderful, absolutely, but what more?"

What more? I searched my memory, but what more could I say? Had I not said all that there was to say? Fé intended to prove a point; she intended to lead me to the answer that she wanted me to discover and realize is my own, but—what more? She waited. I closed my eyes, listening to the music once more. I walked down this hall in hope that I could return to see Za'ara, in hope that the atrium door would still be available to me, but it was not. Instead, I came to meet an alternative version of myself in a mirror. The mirror. When Fé had first shown me the vision, I had said that I wished I could free her. I could free her; even more than that, she had no worry that I would. I felt like that of a child learning similar lessons—the same lessons—again and again and each time feeling as though it had only been the first introduction. I continued to experience many unique things but kept nothing from them. Of course she had frustration with me; I had frustration with myself. Then there was a sharp crack.

I looked to the top corner of the mirror, and there it was. Beautiful, radiant, like a wonderful diamond had come loose from the mirror and danced upon its shining surface. *Crack.*

Fé saw it as well, and she straightened her spine. "Tell me, what more? Why did you intend to return to the atrium?"

"What more…I wanted to return because I have come to realize, even more so, what I am to do. There was a reason that Za'ara was the first to host me. I fought against doubt, against fear, and she enabled me to continue to do so. The terrible things I saw in that room and in the stone cavern; though I act in indifference, my entire being has been undeniably shaken. The transformation that I am undergoing, it is more than one person can endure. See, I am shedding myself of who I once was to enable myself to become who I must. I intended to go to the atrium to be reassured that all that I am doing is right."

Crack. The diamond line in the mirror traveled farther.

Fé watched as it moved and sang, "You want answers. Here is what I must tell you. That of all the things you can become in the world that you speak of, becoming yourself is truly the most precious gift. Yes, you will become caught in storms of doubt and fear, but that is trivial. Might the storm keep you from your destination? Yes! And such is its reason for being. Should you allow it to have such effect? Not if you truly want to arrive where you must be. Let me tell you this. To speak of the majority is to speak of the surface. Do you intend to live life on the surface? I surely hope not! Look to those who lost their voices, those who sat in the atrium. Only during the storm of absolution may they speak; they had no depth, no hope! The majority sits on the surface, but you, and the others who choose to undergo such tremendous self-deconstruction, can live life truly fulfilling their purpose, but first, you must have a voice and words worth speaking."

Yes. This is what I wanted; this is what I needed. The truth. My mind dashed wildly; it was set on fire, and my heart burned furiously with inexorable passion.

"So then, a moment ago when I left the stone cavern, when I danced—I understand. The joy that filled me with such freedom, it was the only reassurance I needed." I smiled; we smiled at one another, for we finally had reconnected. "I do not need others to confirm that I am on the right path. That is for me to know all on my own because it is my own. If I had only listened to the still small voice within me, the one that has brought me to this place, then I would not be filled with such lack of faith in my ability to continue forward." Another crack danced on the silver surface of this great reflecting mirror.

"And to that, what must we ask?" Fé stared at me intently; her brown eyes widened, brimmed with tears.

And my reflection matched hers, and to her answer, I confidently spoke, "What more?"

9

———— ❄ ————

THE TEMPERATURE IN the hall had dropped, not in a drastic way but in a way that was noticeable. Fé and I stood staring at one another through the mirror that was beginning to break. We both wore demeanors of peace, and, finally, we began to resemble one another in more than a physical sense. She was more than a representation of what I could become; she was a promise made to me by all that I had experienced in my life, a compilation of all the lessons learned and adhered to. She was the self that slept silently within me, steering me towards the silver lining of self-worth and accomplishment. Fé was all that I wanted to become.

"You finally understand?"

I nodded, somewhat ashamed. "Yes. I believe that I finally do."

"Then you realize the significance in me asking 'what more?'"

"I believe so."

"Then tell me, I need to make sure that you are on the right path."

I continued, "I admitted that I was uncomfortable with shedding those things of my past, but I also acknowledge that such sacrifice and inner confrontation is necessary for me to begin my journey toward that which I so greatly want to become. It is only human to anticipate the future, and because we are human, we want to leave our marks on history, in nature, or in the minds and hearts of others. To do so, though, we must know that it is crucial to leave behind so much only to move forward and gain so much more. It is not the question of *why* or *how* that we should be asking but instead, that of 'what more?' What more must we do? Whether it breaks us completely or whether it introduces us to parts of ourselves that we were never brave enough to know."

Crack. The anxiety that had been built up in my chest was breaking and dwindling away. I could no longer hear the music of the violin, nor could I smell the flowers fading essence. I felt new. Often I felt as though some things of the past could not be undone; I carried this unease, and it suffocated me, as though everyone knew that I was a fraud. It will happen again. The majority will not understand the minority, and even when our voices find the perfect phrase, the many will disregard it and retreat back unto the surface.

I would rather drown in the truth than be suffocated by mediocrity. I looked at Fé and asked, "And in regards to Maelzer, to his ultimate purpose. He taught a lesson, but his method as a host differed much from that of the methods of Za'ara."

Fé cleared her throat and kept her hands at her side, "Well, there is a reason of course, just as there are reasons for everything that you will encounter. Some reasons bring about greater clarity than others; some just add detail to the larger picture. The details though make the picture all the more grand; the details are how we truly label a work of art by the name of masterpiece."

I furrowed my brow, trying to process all that she said then remarked, "How does that particularly apply to Maelzer?"

"Well, are you not a masterpiece? He, as the deceiver and trickster that he is, was trying to manipulate your details. Not the details that sit on your surface, upon your skin, but the ones that sit in your spirit, your soul, your mind, and your overall well-being. Without these seemingly insignificant details, you would fail to remain yourself."

How remarkable; I am to look at myself and at others as though we are masterpieces embodied. Then I remembered the piece that hung on the wall behind the curtains that had already been placed on the stone wall. "That piece, the piece that was signed with the name Maelzer, how did it come to be? It had not been there before. When I smashed the half sphere, after the shadows fled, then that was when it sat displayed upon the wall."

"Yes, the detail is quite amazing, but is not that which was depicted all the more amazing? The bright sun, casting away the shadow of darkness. Your ability to see past the fog of manipulation that he was preparing to have swallow you whole. Well, you cast the fog away with the amount of self-consciousness you displayed. Your mind and your persona were not susceptible to his ruse. You can fool a fool, but never can you fool one who has learned to be weary of his own shadow."

Fé never failed to amaze me, for everything she had such wonderful insight and spoke with such charm and wisdom. If she is what I am to become, then why would I have any doubt at all? I laughed. "This place. It is extraordinary. Have I been uneasy, yes, I would be a liar if I said otherwise, but truly, the more that I come to experience, the many more questions I come to have! Yet, I have learned so much. The less I know about this place, the more that I come to learn about myself. It is as though this place is directly correlated and is catering to that of my very own mind."

The diamond-encrusted crack that had begun to lattice upon the mirror's surface spread farther; it moved forward in all directions. Light shone out from the silver spaces, and it shed beams upon the hallway and my face. It was brilliant. It danced upon my cheeks, making beautiful shapes and illuminations. I smiled and laughed, "Fé! How very significant this is! I am both my greatest asset and my most potent downfall. I am worthy of the world, and it too is worthy of me. One is not greater than the other."

The abundant grace of understanding kissed the top of my head, and I was consumed by indescribable happiness. There is so much hope, there is worthiness; and though the days may be bleak and our spirit sorrowed, greater is the promise of tomorrow. Today is but a movement, and I choose to move forward with joy in my heart and peace in my mind. The mirror continued to shatter; diamonds rained from the fissures that moved faster still, skating upon the ice of the reflecting mirror.

Another good-bye was to be made, but this good-bye held no sadness, only joy; for everything that I had seen in Fé was now instilled in me. The vision she shared with me, it was no more than pictures but the symbolism was inspiring. In it I stood, on the streets crowded by faces that had no names, and to them I proclaimed, "My lungs, they are not filled with anything other than filth and decay, but you, you are the hope, and hope will rise; so then too will you!" No one turned to look at me; no one seemed to listen, but no such ignorance could harden my uplifted heart, for I had found my one purpose—the greatest lesson of all. I knew myself, that Fé was inside of me, and together, we would sculpt ourselves into the stone of their hearts and plant the seeds that would one day beautifully multiply.

Fé is faith, the faith that I had been lacking my entire life and now, only by looking through a mirror and seeing myself reflected in it, had I been able to see that I had had it all along. In me sat dormant potential; either it could wallow uselessly within me, accomplishing not a thing, or I could stir it, master it, and make unspeakable change. I choose to defend myself against the very things that I fear the most; if sacrifice is all that I must make, then surely I shall ask, what more?

The mirror was splitting wildly; the beams of light danced upon the walls, reflecting off the pieces of art that sat framed in rims of gold. The hallway had fallen silent, the light danced, and with awe, I admired. Fé stood on the other side smiling, and she danced in angelic laughter. She knew that she was free. I reveled in her delight and tilted my head back, basking in the wonderful reality of now. Though I had an idea of what this place was, and though the thought of it alarmed me, I did not allow the worry to overcome me. Many obstacles will cross our paths, sending us astray, whether it be one time alone, or time again times seven. The path is sure, but our feet are not; even knowing this, we will undoubtedly find our way.

Fé stopped dancing and stepped closer to the deteriorating mirror. Her eyes illuminated pure bliss. I stepped closer too, the light still dancing all around us, and she said, "The worry that you had carried, it is not yours but of the world. The stipulations that it has forged has put you and many others in places of depression and lackluster. You blame yourself because what hand but your own could cause such heartache? Do not be deceived, the majority has believed this manipulation, and consequentially they have fallen. The fallen may rise. Have you not risen? It is not the world that must change but our hearts. Progress cannot be made if the individual does not first set the example. This is the cause of so much distress, the root of insurmountable loss. Be first, but do not cheat those who have been made last."

I knew that I did not have much time left with Fé; the mirrored wall was continuously crumbling from its regal stature, and diamonds were falling to the floor then melting away as though made of water. The temperature had dropped more; shivers ran from my spine to my nose. I was freezing cold. With chattering teeth I asked, "Are there more rooms that I will encounter? When will I be able to return home?"

She wrapped her arms around her body and exhaled air that carried flakes of ice. "You are the sole determiner of the time elapsed in this place, and you will return when you know that it is the proper time."

"I am to determine this?"

"Yes, just as you have determined the places that you have already been and the amount of time that you have spent in each place."

"That is something that I have done?"

"Yes, and you will do it again and perhaps again until you have come to a certain place; then after, you will be able to return home."

"By my own hand my path is written. Will there be a sign?"

She laughed and threw her arms far out and twirled. "Do you not see? There are signs in everything we do, in every place we go! The question is: Will you recognize such signs when you see them? Humans are so very attentive to their senses: to sight, hear, smell, taste, and touch."

I bit on the side of my lip and looked around to everything that decorated the hallway; the extravagant rug, the various pieces of art, the rays of light that swayed on the wall, and the dancing diamonds. To say that there was nothing out of the ordinary would be untrue. Everything that was in this place, if questioned, would become more unnatural than it had already seemed. To look at a flower and simply call it a flower was to devalue its truly incredible nature. Then there were those things that I had seen that meaning could not be applied to, for if it had been assigned a name, then its wonder would be made less than it truly was. To live by only that of the senses is to limit one's understanding and more so, hinder the profound ability to access the imagination. If one cannot imagine, then how much less able is he to accept that of the supernatural? To be human—at least in regards to that of my own mind—is to explore the parts of ourselves that are beyond that of explanation. Have you not sat and thought, *Well surely it would be a dream of all dreams to be capable of the impossible* then later find yourself doing just that which you had previously believed could only be a dream? Surely, this I could not deny.

I did not doubt the unnatural; I had entertained it through that of novels and daydreams. I would become lost in thought thinking of that which the many had told me could not come true, yet in subtle sensitivity I would not take their word. I looked to Fé, who had become distracted by the lights that shined on the mirror, and urged, "If I were to limit my senses, then, would this allow me to be more impressionable to that of the unnatural? It has, without doubt and on multiple occasions, happened that I have seen figures from the corner of my eye but do not believe that which I know I have seen."

"Then that would point again to the world."

"But has not the world inspired fairytales, that of creature and beast?"

"But they have not accepted it as truth. It is one thing to entertain that of the imagination but another to accept it."

"How could such be true? The very ideas that they dream of, would they be so selfish as to choose mediocrity and deny such intimacy? How profoundly beautiful would it be to share your most personal philosophical ideologies with those who wish to know you in ways more tender than that of skin and touch."

"Such is the way of the world, is it not? There are those who fear that their voices have no effect; they deem tales that they wish were truth to that of folklore."

I closed my eyes, searching my mind for an answer. To such a sentiment, I could relate. Many times I have not spoken when I believed that I should; I have not stood for that which I believed wholeheartedly. The feeling that I am left with after the moment of juncture has been lost; it is as though a disaster has struck, stealing opportunity away from those who may have needed intervention the most. I sighed and spoke thoughtfully, "It would be beautiful. If we were only willing to submit to the greater cause that each of us individually has. When the words sit on our heart, that is when we should share them. The words need not be profound, for each of us has a unique manner in expressing ourselves; the act, all on its own, would be more than enough. It is not the power of the word but the strength of the tongue that makes all the difference."

I knew that I would not have company for much longer now; Fé knew as well. We stood there in silence as we watched the barrier fall closer to its breaking point. There was serenity in the atmosphere even though the light danced wildly upon the walls, making it hard to see. The diamonds would fall out from the cracks of the mirror and melt away into the carpeting. The diamonds, streaking down so beautifully on the silver mirror, resembled tears falling down the faces of angels; and though I might never speak such a statement, the sight did indeed evoke wonderful enchantment.

I approached the mirror and gently placed the palm of my hand against its fragile surface; to this gesture Fé spoke, "Do not worry. Everything will fall into place, and once it does, you will only know happiness. You are on the right path toward every one of your heart's desires." She knew me so intimately, in ways that I had never expressed to another living soul.

I stretched my fingers further on the glass, keeping my eyes on hers. "I am not worried. If anything, I am comforted. For the first time in my life, I am understood for every aspect of myself; even more, I am accepted regardless of my many downfalls. You are the muse that my art has longed for and I the reason that it has also suffered. No longer."

"You have no idea the magnificent peace you have given me; I have a future now. For so long I narrowly evaded the darkness of our own insecurities. Seeing you now, knowing that you will become that which will welcome me. You have given me life. Surely we shall prevail, even if only we find strength enough to lift our eyes toward the horizon. Another day has been promised, life will be made anew, and so shall we."

Tears brimmed at the edges of my eyes. My eyelashes blinked them away, and with my left hand I wiped beneath my nose; I composed myself. I stood tall with my shoulders rolled back; my chin was not hung low nor was it held up into the air. The tears that sat in my eyes were not of pain or sorrow but of utter respect and gratitude. I had only now, in these young years of my adult life, come to know myself. I stared at myself through the shattered mirror wall, my hand still calmly set upon it. I had finally come to terms with myself. Knowing who I am and what I intended to become—I would not have to lie to others. No longer would I need to be more clever, to portray something that I was not. I would not need to shrug away from human contact or their words of comfort. Arrogance was not a characteristic of the strong. I had always been a misrepresentation of the latest human struggle, lacking originality and passion, but now I knew; with weary steps I would heed my shadow, avoiding the fall that has captured the many.

I was my own greatest asset, my own most wonderful companion; through Fé I was able to interact with a part of myself that I was unsure I could ever unlock without the reinforcement of self-awareness. I brought my consciousness back to my hand, and Fé stood on the other side. She smiled and reached her hand toward mine, placing it adjacent to the mirror. With a brave tongue she spoke, "You are never alone; I am a part of you for always; look within and there you will find me." Our eyes connected for a brief moment; then with great force, I pushed my hand through the mirrored wall, and down it came falling. Shards of mirror fell musically to the ground, and diamonds escaped through the cracks and were tossed into the air. The image of my face danced around me in the reflection of the many mirror pieces, and with light thuds, they all landed upon the carpet.

The remnants of the wall lay on the ground; the diamonds had melted away and were now water stains upon the carpet. Though for a moment I wished to mourn, I did no such thing. Instead I placed my hand on my heart and inhaled deeply; faith was within me. Knowing this, I carefully stepped over the shards and stains so that they would not come to contact with my bare feet. I should be exhausted, but I was not; I was encouraged, for I knew that much more was ahead. Epiphany had graced my spirit, and forward I went with confident steps. Whatever may be before me, I would look upon it with wisdom and poise, and to that which I did not understand I would ask "what more?" I knew that the secrets of this journey had only just truly begun to reveal themselves.

10

———— ❊ ————

THE ONLY DIRECTION I could move was forward.
The mirror had fallen, as well as the barrier that I
had kept strong within the walls of my heart, and
although I was more vulnerable to that of fallacious attack,
I too was more able to counter every attempt that fought
to dismantle my defenses. I knew that great things were to
come. I looked ahead then turned to look back. I did not
detect any ill-mannered forces and was eager to move diligently onward. I looked to my feet; how thankful I was for
them, for they have taken me many places, and to many more
we will go. There was still debris from the shattered mirror
wall on the ground, and near that pile was a single diamond;
it had not melted away like the others had. It was stunning.
I walked over to where it laid and I kneeled down to exam-
ine it closer. Gently I picked it up and held it between my
thumb and index finger; it was approximately the size of a
dime, and its design was of its natural form: raw and uncut.

I admired it so. Although I was a woman, and a young one at that, I had not yet come to the age where I had longed for one of my own. Never did I deny the beauty of such gems; simply I had just not come to terms with all that they required me to part with, at least not at this point in time of my life. First, I must know myself, and when that time came, then I would be able to know another. The diamond, notably one of the most exquisite gems to grace the ring fingers of many women, was a gem to be received rather than taken. This diamond though was perhaps the most simple of all that I had seen, rough in texture and triumphant in its creation; in my eyes, that made it the most beautiful of all indeed. It did not have a significant shine to it; truth be told, it was rather dull in luster. I looked around on the floor but saw no others like it.

I held the diamond between my fingers for a moment longer, deciding whether to lay it back down or bring it along with me. I closed my eyes; I would take it. An object of such beauty should not be left amongst the rubble. Though this contradicted my previous thought, I knew that the decision to have such a possession would benefit me in one way or another. I stood up with this precious stone in my hand; my nightdress did not have any pockets, so I had to improvise. This dress was no longer suitable and would most definitely be discarded once I returned home; it has ultimately served its purpose. I tore a piece of fabric away from the very bottom of the hemline; I was careful to not tear it off completely though. Once there was a sufficient amount of fabric torn away, I delicately placed the raw diamond onto the cloth and rolled it; then after, I tied the piece of fabric into a knot. It did not look rather silly at all. I shook my leg as to test the durability of my makeshift safehold. It held quite nicely and seemed to be secure. I was proud of my small accomplishment and once again focused my attention forward.

The hall had not changed, but the lighting seemed to be somewhat dimmer; perhaps, if anything, my eyes were just simply strained or extremely exhausted from all that they have been asked to see. I had not kept track of how much time had passed since I had first entered this phenomenon. It felt as though days had passed, but such could not be; if anything, this journey had just been that of hours. The passing of time did not preoccupy me. How much time had I wasted in the years past? Countless; hours more would not be detrimental, especially when such time is being spent in a place that challenges your entire known self. Then a light flickered from the direction of my peripheral vision. That must be the way I should now go. I continued walking forward.

This hall was an ever-changing maze. When I was least prepared, change would occur. My spirit was strong; it had faith that anything that could come would not deter me from that which I wanted most. I reached toward the hem of my dress to make sure that the raw diamond had not been lost; it was still safe there. Another light flickered. Strange, the ceiling of the hall did not have visible light fixtures installed. The same had been in the atrium. There was light but no direct source of it, at least not to the naked eye; even so, it could not be refuted that though the source of the light was unknown, there was light nonetheless. Again, another light flashed for a second, then it returned, shining just as it had before. I continued to walk forward and then stopped. The exotic Turkish rug—I could see the end of it. I had walked on it for so long, but never had I seen it reach its end. Even when the hall ended behind the mirror, the carpet had simply continued to run, but now, I could see the carpets decorative fringe as it had clearly come to an end. As though right on cue, the omniscient presence within called me forward. There was only dim lighting ahead, and I was not easily able to determine what awaited me in the obscure distance. I readied myself and continued into the unknown with sure steps. Two, four, six.

My bare feet took their last steps on the extravagantly detailed carpet, and right as my toes edged guardedly near the fringe, I took a breath and prepared myself. With faith, I took a step forward. The ground now felt like that of a concrete sidewalk, coarse but not necessarily unpleasant. There was minimal lighting, and I was unable to clearly see the length of more than four steps ahead. I kept calm; what would come would be no more than further preparation for my restored spirit. I would be tested constantly. My mind must become impenetrable to that of the world, to its influences. I had already learned that the majority could not touch me unless I became cold toward that of my own agenda. Another light flickered quickly, then the great darkness of my past darted across the hall to another hidden corner. Again it returned. Its timing had always been ideal, but I refused to fall prey to any inconceivable demon of fear, for I was greater than that that wished to destroy me.

My body sought to pause, to stop, but my heart would not allow it such exemption. Although my body was frail, easily inclined to temptation and malady, it should be urged to continue always. I kept my chin up, facing the direction in which I intended to go. The entity dashed across the hallway, latching onto the walls with scratching claws. I wanted to run, to escape, but a demonstration done in such haste would only encourage this monstrosity to prolong his hellish behaviors. Two, four, six. This being, the same one that I had seen in the warehouse, was not of this world. Perhaps I had slipped into its world; this could very well be his wicked domain. No, he had resided as well in my own home, had traveled behind me to the many places that I had gone during my routine errands. My eyes did not blink nor did they look away from where they intended to go.

The lights flickered—on then off then on again. The dark, it had always made me somewhat uneasy. This being, it must know. The temperature was the lowest that it had been; my breath would escape from my mouth with harsh licks of ice. Then the lights went out completely. Complete abyss. I closed my eyes in attempt to console myself. Two, four, six. I heard this manifestation leaping from wall to wall; the sound came closer. It sounded as though the integrity of this hall was falling apart, being brought violently down. I stood motionless on the concrete sidewalk floor; not a muscle moved, not a breath was made, and not one of us stirred. This was not of my own mind. Such a creature was not the making of cognate fear or the chilling notions of an imagination gone rampant. He would not stay long; never did he stay long. He must not thwart my efforts.

I lifted my left arm forward and my right arm to the side. My eyes remained closed. I knew that he lurked in the darkness; he would only stalk me with his devilish vision, but as for attacking me—no, never, he would not dare. I swayed both arms slowly around me to ensure that nothing blocked my way of walking. There was scratching against the wall, then there was a crash. My body jumped, but my eyes still stayed closed shut. A picture frame must have fallen from its place on the wall. My fingertips were frozen, terrified that they would come into contact with that of the horrific presence of this unknown existence. Two, four, six.

He continued to make his presence known. Of the many times I had encountered him, such methods had not been exercised; but this time, his taunting was acted out with noticeable aggression. He was frantic.

Then there was a deep sob of deplore; it rang in my ear drums, causing my body excruciating pain. I hunched my spine forth, bending in an aching way, and covered my ears, refusing to open my shut eyes. I had held them closed for so long that I began to see streaks of bright color rushing behind my eyelids. I so very much wanted him to leave. He cried out in a horrible bellow, and it echoed throughout the length of the hall. The wail bounced off the walls, and then there was a sound that for my entire life I will not be able to forget, though I wish I could—there was diabolical laughter. In a moment of dread and desperation, I believed that I had only imagined such a nerve striking sound, but, no. The laughter had been audible. No words had been said by this animal-mimicking being, no clear intention had been revealed, but one thing was irrefutable: this stalking beast had a distinct purpose of his very own as well.

I nearly had no strength at all to lift my body from the position that shock had bent it into. From my earliest memories of childhood, I recall being lectured by a wagging finger. I had known that there were things that we had been taught to call good and those that we learned to call bad. As children, we were not trained to question those things that we are shown. That spoken by a tongue more mature than our own was accepted as truth. Those who did raise their tongues to ask questions of the age refined, well, they were labeled as bold but were also degraded, called by names such as *depraved* and *rebellious*. Such children were not made leaders; they were made examples. Examples to the other children who had seen them find their voice. Such was the way of the world, and such ways have not yet been done away with.

Not I though; I had been favored and raised in a household that encouraged such inquisitiveness. My inquisitive nature had become a characteristic of myself that I was very much glad to have. Now, in this hall accompanied by that which could be nothing else but of another world, I asked myself this question: Of the many things that could be accomplished in this unnamed place, what did I have that must be so very precious, that he so fervently wished to rob of me? It was true that he appeared only when my spirit had been lifted and my heart encouraged. The many times I had laid in my bed, sleepless, unable to shake myself of the intolerable ache caused by the human condition, he did not appear. Never did he appear when my spirit was already irrevocably broken. A thief, he was. Only when I found worth in this life did he wake and come forth from the shadows, causing me to ultimately question all that I had been taught, all that I knew was of evil and of good.

He too, though dark and monstrous, had purpose, and such was to rob me of my own by inviting fear to return to the forefront of my mind after I had battled so meticulously to cast it away.

What purpose would a victory made in his name serve? If I were to succumb to the forces that he violently thrust upon me, what then would his purpose be? I had since been able to lift my body into an upright position, still cautious of him who watched from the shadows; my eyes were still closed. I could not fear that which I could not see; even more, I could not fear that which I understood. For this reason, if for no other reason at all, was the purpose of those who had trained the minds of the young. They held the absolute power. To be a teacher is to mold those minds that would be influenced by all that they have seen; their ability to see what is around them would not serve the best interest of the majority, not at all. For the majority do as they please and will continue to do as they wish for all of their lives, and thus are born such figures of language much like this. See what they do, but do not do that which you have seen, for you must do as you are told and do so with no question on your tongue.

If I may speak for myself, I will not permit my tongue to sit quietly, or comfortably, in conformity. When my tongue does speak to challenge and question those who wish to silence me, I pray that it would be favored, for speaking that which could break down the barriers set upon the few by the many who act in selfishness and greed would only cause an amazing ripple effect. And as for this entity of filth! I did not welcome it any longer; its presence did not evoke fear but only that of frustration and intolerance. I had continued walking, though I knew not exactly where I went, eyes shut and arms spread out. He leapt from wall to wall, lunging from place to place; his hellish claws would screech against the concrete, causing a noise so incredibly sickening. He did not laugh again; he roared. He was in fury, yet I had faith that he would not cause me any harm.

I stopped walking and purposefully stood confidently in place; with a brave tongue, I spoke, "I will not fear you! You have failed; you will not reach my heart!" I held my breath. His claws did not scrape against the concrete; there was no movement—silence. I released the air that I was holding in my lungs. Then, upon my face, was a breath. It was steaming hot and smelled of death; I cringed, and in my throat was a dry gag that caused me to choke. Nausea sat uneasily at the pit of my stomach; the colors behind my eyelids raced at speeds that made me dizzy. And again, this entity laughed in a way so diabolical that my knees could not help but buckle. Sickness. Disease. No. Two, four, six. I would not fall. After his laughter ceased, the silence returned again. With my hand, I wiped away the putrid sensation of saliva and death that sat on my face. I forced back a dry heave.

I straightened my spine. I must continue; more was awaiting me, and he wanted nothing else but to keep me from that which I must experience. He believed with his evil spirit that I had seen quite enough. With my eyes still shut closed, I walked forward and confessed, "You have no power over me." Though it could almost not be determined whether I spoke in confession or that in a way to convince myself of such proclamation, that detail did not matter, for the first most important step was to speak at all. I stepped forward, one hand still upon my face and the other wrapped around my trim torso. At that instant I heard a bloodcurdling voice. No, not a voice, but voices—multiple voices. Many of them spoke at the same time, I could not count how many exactly, but they all came from the same source. Saying that to hear such horror was mortifying would be an understatement. I could not put into words the unspeakable resounding abhorrence that his intonation triggered. Worse of all, the most horrible detail was not merely the sound of his demon voice, but that which he spoke.

He laughed, growled, spit, and taunted, "If I do not have any power, then why, human, do you refuse to open your eyes to see me?"

Two, four, six. My eyes rolled behind my eyelids, my head pounded, and with all of my strength, I stayed standing. Not one flinch was made, not one adjustment of a pinky finger. Frozen. I dare not admit that he tempted fear to enter my heart; never would I grant him such flattery. I had nothing more to say but to repeat that which I had already spoken, "You have no power over me." I waited for him to respond; it felt as though I waited an eternity, but it could not have been longer than that of a minute or so. Persistently, I began to take steps forward. I had been kept from everything that I needed the most out of this life by him—by him who evoked fear and doubt. It was he, since my childhood, who would watch me from high, hidden corners. He would see me seeing him, and thus was his pleasure; it pleased him so to see that his presence had great effect on me. Now, being more bold and self-aware, his presence did not provoke all that it had so easily in the past. That must be the only reason that he had to come closer and more aggressively than he ever had in the past.

If anything, by him doing so, it was a reflection that I had indeed come great lengths. When I had met him in the warehouse, the language of my body could do nothing else but confirm that he still held immense power over me. Presently, I resisted every urge to fall victim to the vehement behavior that he displayed. I had reinforced myself and everything that I stood for; with unconditional certitude, I represented all that I knew I wanted of this world: hope, bravery, self-assurance, worth, and, perhaps greatest of all, love of self. If I had become more steadfast, then too must he, and such attribute he did display by pronouncing his presence all the more belligerently. I should not be at all afraid. To come to realize that your enemy has become more aggressive is only an indication that you, as an individual, are on the path to that which your heart desires. Is it not your enemy who watches you closely to warrant your failures?

It was so astounding to me to be thrust into a place of nonverifiable existence and be begrudgingly cast into a process of thought that made me confront every aspect of myself. Such a process was not to comfort me but to challenge me. Very few would willingly undergo such a grueling, humiliating, mutilation of self; only very few would be compliant. In everything that I did, there was further evidence that I was to be called upon, that for some reason, I could be used for a greater good. This being, his voice did not intimidate the voice that sat still in my spirit; it would not keep mine from rising either. More boldly now, I raised my voice louder yet, daring the entity to challenge me once more. "Did you hear me?" I said spitefully, "You have no power over me!" I listened; I heard the sound of the air moving within the hall. The temperature was still frigid; there was an odor of death in the air, like that of a carcass. His claw would get caught in the wall, and he would pluck it out clumsily.

I waited. I knew he heard; he heard everything that I said, even that which had not even fallen from my mouth.

His omniscience allowed him passage of my mind. Truth be told, I had never denied him. Of course he was impetuously vying for my attention; never had I forbid him my ear. Although then—then I was a different person, I was not the same young woman that stood here, impudently resisting his lure into darkness. I was not stagnant as I had been before. I could only imagine—and how awful it must have looked—myself lying corpselike on my bed motionless, tossed into another bought of depression, questioning my very existence, and apologizing for every breath of air that I stole from others who were more deserving. I shuddered. How dismal I had been, accepting every falsehood that he had whispered into my ear. Now he sees that I am a different woman; he knows. And because he recognizes this truth, he must exercise other forms of blandishment, for his lies no longer seduced me.

And then a response. From the walls, his multitoned murmur fell down from right above me. "Then open your eyes to see me." His lure did not entice me. I felt his fiendish breath upon the scalp of my head; he had hung above me all this time. Open my eyes to see him. I had seen him before.

The sight of him still elicited discomfort; when I saw him, the reality of my fragile humanity rang true. He was a large creature, seven feet in height, shaped like that of a wolf ready to pounce, but he had not the face of a wolf.

His face was still that of a mystery to me. It was like that of Maelzer; it existed but it was not prominent or defined by particular features. His claws were bearlike, with ankles of a dog. Disproportioned by nature's laws, he should be unable to leap so agilely in great distances, but this creature did not adhere to the laws of nature. He did not take steps; he stalked, he avoided the ground always, and he much preferred to dwell within the corners where the walls met the ceiling. His spine was arched, his torso wide, his waist thin, and his haunches were of pure muscle. Though the sight of him was unworldly and disgustingly disturbing, it was his presence that was most unpleasant. His presence would somehow provoke my memory, inviting me to recall all my past failures, every shortcoming, each lie, and each heartbreak. It was my weaknesses that he sought to highlight. In our human weakness he is able to find his greatest victories.

I was merely mortal; my lifespan ticked and ran ahead of me. A thing such as time would wait for no one. This I knew, for he had encouraged death to me in the days gone by; never did I entertain his perverse notions on a grand scale. On a lesser and more so generalized scale, yes, and now that I have learned that the details of a man are what makes him a masterpiece, I am able to recognize that even entertaining the smallest of his implications were detrimental to my mental and emotional well-being. My eyes had already grown so tired and had begun to twitch. I knew that I could not continue to strain them, so I prepared to open them to acknowledge his presence. He lurked above me, so I inclined my head backward and faced the ceiling with shut eyes. I felt his exhalation upon my face, and I winced. Two, four, six. With a sudden reflex, I opened my eyes to see nothing at all.

I kept my head back and first searched the ceiling; he was gone. I shifted my body swiftly to check behind me, but there was no sign of his presence. I was relieved. My spirit was at ease, but calmly it issued warning; I would need to continue to practice mental preparation, for it was inevitable that I would cross paths with him again. I looked to the ground; I still stood on the concrete sidewalk. This I had known; my feet ached and were embedded with tiny stones that scratched the bottom of their sensitive heels. I reached down to wipe them away., knowing that I would only step on them again. Finally, I looked to my surroundings. There had been quite a change during the time I had walked forward with my eyes shut. The walls were now lined with red brick. They were not new, not old, just somewhat faded and tired. There were lights fixed on the top part of the wall, like those that you would see on a public street. It became clear to me that I was no longer in the lavish hall that had led me to so many places.

This was an alleyway, mucky and dim. I rubbed my eyes as to allow them to adjust and looked once more at my surroundings. I was alone again. He had left just as he always had. Next time, I would be ready. I had acted in defiance to his presence but not in unquestionable bravery. Much was left to be learned, and through my experiences I knew that I would only become more ready to defend myself from such an animal. I reached down, and my raw diamond was still in place. I twisted my body and stretched, lifted my arms to fluff my hair, then moved with my ring finger to bend my eyelashes up. I walked forward confidently, humming the tune that had been sung by the half sphere in the room before.

11

THE ALLEYWAY WAS nothing out of the ordinary. It was similar to those that you would find behind local strip malls in your hometown. Brick on both walls, coarse sidewalk, dim lighting; there did not seem to be anything that struck me as particularly odd. Something would turn up though; something always had. I continued to walk in an even pace. I did not want to rush forward and miss a factor of importance. There was still that same smell in the air as before—of carcass. It was not potent, but the odor did come with a bit of sting to it, and it was not one of pleasantry. The temperature was still cold; it has not been this cold some paces back. There was a howl of the wind, and, for a moment, I thought that it said "go." I shook my head and massaged my temple in small circular motions. My mind was exhausted; it had not been allowed rest. Both physically and emotionally, I was drained. There had been so many various components to this journey; each required an enormous portion of attention due to the intricacies of each place that I had been led to. The energy that I had been required to dispel had been the most that I had used in such a long time, not to mention that level of mindfulness that was needed to accurately embrace each lesson taught by the host.

It was imperative that my mind stay sharp. If my awareness was to dwindle, then so would my capability to meet the conditions of each room. I thought back to the places that I had been. It had not been that long ago, but time did not elapse here as it did at home. The warehouse, the atrium, the stone cavern, and the reflecting mirror; each room had its own lesson, and each lesson applied to a flaw of my character. *Flaw* might not be the proper word to use; for each characteristic that a person can have, there is both a positive and a negative contribution. To each of my own, both aspects had been reflected and elaborated upon in each room. It was difficult to digest all that I had been told. I acted with intelligence to everything that had been told to me, yet I was unsure how such words could even be my own. To the statements and responses that came from my mouth, well, some of them shocked even myself. I was unable to understand how they could even belong to me. When it came to the topic of expressing my opinion, such had never been my forte.

I thought back to Fé, how in our conversation we referred to those who act as witnesses to situations that should be intervened in rather than only observed. If such a case were tried by court, I would be found guilty, reckless even. What a shame to know that wrong is being done but not to have courage enough to counsel. The odor became stronger, and in the air was the taste of iron. I did not want to swallow, but I had no other choice. Iron—it tasted of blood, and immediately I wished to spit it out but did not. There was something up ahead on the ground. I could not make out what it was exactly, but soon enough, with a couple more steps, I would be able to see. There was a change in the atmosphere, and, faintly, I could hear the drone of conversation. People. There must be another room up ahead. People? I had not yet seen a group of people in this place, at least not a crowd. The atrium had been the place where I had encountered the highest volume of company, and that was only five individuals in total, including myself. People.

I hurried forward. I was eager to see where the crowd was and to discover why they accumulated there. On the ground, there was something bold. I kept walking forward and stood in front of what lay on the concrete. It was spray paint; the bright color yellow was painted across the width of the concrete sidewalk in the hue that expressed caution. Along it were forward and backward slashes in deep black that outlined the message that was painted in the striped center: "Watch your step." It was in the print that would be used in the vicinity of a construction site. Before I took a step forward, I again evaluated my surroundings. Nothing, not one thing was seemingly out of place. Heeding the message, I proceeded with caution. With anticipation, I quickly turned behind me, but there was not a thing there either. I moved forward, and on the ground again was another message on the concrete identical to the one that I had just seen: "watch your step."

Although there was nothing too alarming about this alleyway, I adhered to that which was written. Nothing changed in this place except for the temperature and the odor; both grew more unbearable. Ahead, I could see that the same signage was painted on the ground. With a brisk jog, I ran up to it. It read the same: "watch your step." I grew more curious. The buzz of the crowd became louder; there must be an entire room filled with people. I knew that there must be a new place up ahead, and the thought excited me. I prepared my mind. I paced forward with a light jog for what seemed to be twenty paces, then I quickly halted. To my left there were steps—just three. Three steps that led up to a door. On the left side of these steps was a wrought iron railing; they had minimal detailing, and I found it odd that only that one side of the steps had this accommodation.

The door was of standard make; it looked like the common door that you would find featured at any strip mall location. Silver aluminum border outlined the frosted glass center. It was eerie how ordinary the door was in comparison to everything else that was in this unnatural place. On the center of the door was a sign; it hung at the direct center of the door, hanging from a small adhesive hook. The small sign read Open. Open. It was outlined in the traditional border of red and blue; it was so completely typical that it nearly did not make any sense to me as to why it was possibly there. I looked forward up ahead, but the darkness did not allow me to see; the same could be said about the direction that was left behind me as well. I looked at the door. The conversation of people could be heard from the inside. It was not an overwhelming sound; it did not cast fear or that of excitement. It was just rather ordinary, and the ordinary seemed, if anything, dull to me.

I waited for a couple minutes, fiddling with my hands and nails. "Watch your step." What did this mean exactly? When I walked through this door, would my state of detachment be toppled? Perhaps the written message should not be one that is to be read into but just simply is as it appears: a sign that simply warned me to watch my step. I tried hard to not heavily decipher everything that I encountered. It was one thing to be cautious and another to be paranoid. I took another breath and approached the steps. Three steps up and through a door; the handle was cold to the touch as I pulled it open. The air rushed out as though it was eager for escape. I stepped into the room, and there was a ring; my arrival had been announced.

That which I had come to expect was not at all what was before me. I stood at the entrance of what was, without any doubt, a butcher's shop. The drop in temperature had suddenly begun to make sense. There was a counter that displayed several cuts and styles of meats; the counter was like one that you would see at a deli: not at all extravagant, yet practical in display. The walls were eggshell white, and the tile on the floor matched it. There were shelves with merchandise on the right side of the room, but they were not filled with many product options. There were people. Some people stood in neat lines; there were three lines, and each line had roughly four people in them. Then there were also other people; these people did not stand in line. Unorderly in fashion, they crowded the front of the butcher's counter; there were six people doing this. I watched them to see if I would notice a tendency that I should be tentative of, but they did nothing that caused worry. They seemed to be ordinary people standing in a butcher's shop, awaiting their turn to be serviced.

There was conversation being had; everyone seemed to be speaking, but their lips did not move. I watched their mouths. Chatter was being made; it was distinct, yet as I watched their mouths, they still did not move to shape such speech. The words that found their way to my ears could almost not be understood; yes, it was in a language that I could understand, but for reason beyond my own, I could not. There was no music to be heard like there had been in each of the rooms before, and for the people themselves, they too were rather dull in the most ordinary of ways. There were both males and females. Some waited in line, others did not. There were not features that seemed to be exaggerated either. If I could be quite honest, they were all rather plain. Some wore mustaches, others had curly hair, and some were tall, short, slender, and not; they were simply people all awaiting service.

The odor was very strong now; now that I knew it was the smell of slabs of meat, it made me fairly queasy. My stomach was not meant to handle blood or to work efficiently with aspects of death or gore; the knowledge that the smell came from exposed meat did not settle very well at all. I was still standing near the entrance of the door and had not yet determined where I should go first or to whom I should approach first, so I continued to observe. I watched the counter where the meat was displayed, and behind it was a man. Tall, well-rounded in stature, balding with skin that had a greasy shine, he walked back and forth behind the counter, but I could not see what he was doing. There was a room behind the counter. The walls were the same shade of off–white, and it had a simple entrance without a door. I did not see him go through that entrance nor could I see what was behind it either.

I bit the inside of my lip and pursed my mouth. There must be something that I am missing. I looked to my left and saw a stand; on this stand was a roll that contained numbers—those numbers that were required of us to pull to maintain order in a place. I had always been one to respect order and pulled a number; this way, I would have a spot and not be disrespecting the sequence of service that was being made. I did not look at my number; I just clenched it in my hand. I decided that it was safe to walk forward and approach the people who waited in front of the counter.

No one noticed me, and this did not surprise me. I went to the middle line and stood behind the fourth person. I looked again to my company. There all wore colors and out-fits of different types; there were women in suits and men in belted jeans. Some men wore sandals, and some women wore sundresses. They looked much more normal than I did; no one was wearing a nightdress. I snickered out loud and quickly brought my hand up to cover my mouth. I did not want to bring attention to myself before time allowed. I looked ahead at those who stood in line ahead of me: a hat, brown hair, a bun, no hair. Waiting would serve no purpose, especially if I did not know what I was waiting for. Meat? Were all these people waiting in line for their night's portion of protein for dinner? It was quite odd.

I stepped out of line and approached the counter. There were some people that had done the same; they were not in line, yet they assumed that they would be catered to first. They wore faces of impatience and frustration. One man just stood there with his arms crossed and nodded his head from side to side in a dissatisfied manner. I couldn't help but release a sarcastic scoff. It seemed like he would be waiting for some time more because the man behind the counter did not seem to be serving anyone at all. He just continued to pace back and forth in his work space. I became curious; no one looked at me. Could they see me? I turned around and began to wander around the crowd, weaving in and out of the lines and bumping my shoulders into them as they waited, but no one seemed to be bothered. At this point, all I wanted was a reaction, even one of annoyance.

And where was this place's host? I had always been greeted by a host in a somewhat-timely manner. Why was this time any different? I focused on the room itself again. There were people, some in and out of line, a counter that contained meats, and a butcher that served no meat at all even though there were people anxiously waiting. The scent that resided in the air was horrendous; it caused sickness in my stomach, and I tried hard to take as few breaths as possible. I went and stood near a woman; she had blonde frizzy hair, light green eyes, and a small nose. I stood to her right, shoulder to shoulder, mimicking the way she moved her body. Heel to toe, heel to toe, heel again, stop. Then, she would look to her left wrist to check the time. Perhaps she did not realize where she was yet, that this place did not move with time. I turned my body toward hers and stood on my tiptoes; she was much taller than I was, but then many people were. I brought my face closer to hers—closer, then closer—but she did not budge; I went unnoticed.

I became somewhat frustrated. How was I to learn anything at all if nothing at all was even happening? I sighed heavily. No one heard. I sighed louder in a way that was sarcastic and overdramatic. Perhaps these people were not even people at all, oh, well. I turned back to the blonde lady and said, "Hello, do you hear me?" She obviously did not. I spoke with more authority. "Hello!" Again, I went unnoticed. All the while she moved in the routine that she had done before: heel to toe, heel to toe, heel again, and then a glance to her watch. They must be mannequins, robots, beings without intellect or regard, only inanimate shapes of those who do. I decided to push the boundaries. I extended my right arm up and brought together both my ring and middle finger; I raised my arm to the temple of her head. She had not noticed that I invaded her personal space before, maybe she would not a second time. I gingerly placed my fingers onto the top of her head and could not believe what I witnessed.

It was as though she had abruptly come to life. Her body moved in a more lively way, her lips moved, and she lamented, "Hurry! I have been here for ages, hurry! There are places I must go, people that I must see. Hurry. When will there be another to serve? I am famished. I cannot go where I am destined if I do not get my share first. How much longer? Hurry." I pulled my hand away from her head and leaned back in disbelief. There was now only that which I had heard when I first entered the room, the low buzz of chatter and murmurs. It must not be conversation at all; the sound that filled the shop must be the disembodied thoughts of the many individuals who stood in this room waiting for their turn. Her body still moved in the way that it had before. I held my breath and reached my hand up to touch the top of her head once more.

When I did, she jumped back into liveliness. "Hurry, I have been waiting my turn for so long already. When will I be served?" A knot sat in my stomach, and I began to sweat. How was such a thing even happening? My mouth was dry and tasted of iron; I rolled my tongue over my lips and probed, "How long have you been waiting?"

She turned her head to me and tipped it completely to the side, and then to the other. "What? Why do you need to know? Who are you? Will you serve me?" She freakishly ogled me with wild green eyes, awaiting an answer, but I did not know what answer she expected in return to her unusual questions.

"I am waiting too. I do not need to know the many details; I only would like to know what you are waiting for and if you might happen to know how long that I might be made to wait. What is it that you are waiting to be served?"

She pulled her neck back in offense to everything that I had asked; and bent her neck in a different angle and snapped, "I will wait longer than you will, much longer! I will wait longer than anyone else in this shop. I will wait, and I will be served!" Her overall conduct did not comfort me; the knot in my stomach became tighter.

I kept my fingertips against the top of her head although I no longer wished to interact with her or her internal madness; against my will, I spoke to her again and softly persisted, "I have many places more that I intend to go; I have no doubt that you will wait longer than I will. I have waited long enough. What do you want to be served so badly?"

Sneering disgustingly at me, she jeered, "If you do not know what you are waiting for, then you are certainly someone that I do not consider competition. Leave me be, I do not like you."

Offended, I pulled my hand from this miserable woman. How very rude! She did not answer any of my questions and only spoke of herself. I stepped away from her and watched as she continued her uninteresting routine: heel to toe, heel to toe. She wore an unmoving face of disdain; such was her personality. I could not ask an unwilling ear to hear.

I turned around, deeming the blonde a lost cause, and walked to the shelves that sat at the back of the shop in the right-hand corner. On them sat randomized items that sat in a form of disarray; there were containers, shakers, and jars that were labeled in red marker on top of white tape. These items were not that of a butcher's shop but of a laboratory of anatomical sciences. In these glass jars were various human body parts: eyes, fingers, pieces of flesh. My stomach churned. Of the many things I could handle, the sight of blood or gore was not among them. I gagged cripplingly and fought revoltingly to swallow the sweltering upheave, to keep such vile retch in my empty stomach. If I had had any previous appetite, it was now lost. What was worse was how these jars were labeled. The glass jar that held eyes that had been plucked from a human skull, the optic nerves still attached and floating grotesquely around; on the white tape was written "Twenty-twenty." Could this possibly be referring to the ability of vision that these organs had had previous to their collection?

I placed one hand over my mouth; the other was wrapped around my stomach as to comfort the ache that had fallen upon it. The smell of rotting meat did not help the matter. I cringed at every breath that I had to take, for it left the residue of blood and iron on my tongue. I was disgusted. I looked at the next container: a liver. It did not seem to have been in good health during its lifespan. It was black around its edges, with bruises upon it in deep purple and gray; it must have endured grim ailment. I placed my hand on my stomach; it throbbed at the sight of such a thing. The red marker also named this organ, and on the tape was written

"Hazel." A name? Is this who this liver was stolen from? I shuddered.

I had always preferred books to that of the study of sciences; science limited my imagination, and my creativity had been a hobby that has always given me much insight to those things that I could not explain. Many times, believers of science would cut me down and be quick to diagnose my character, to recommend me to a doctor that would prescribe solutions through medication. Always I would kindly decline such offers. I appreciated the sciences though, particularly the ones of psychology, but never did I study them in pursuance of a career. No, still now, I prefer books and conversations with strangers who do not hold their tongue in regard to their opinions. Life was my most esteemed teacher and my most long-term edification.

I continued to peruse the mason jars that sat upon the tan shelves. Another jar, this time labeled "Distant," held that of a heart no bigger than the size of a fist. I held out my hand and curled it into a fisted shape; it was roughly about the same size as the one that had been stolen and now floated in a place that it could not call home. I lifted my fist to my chest and held it over where my beating heart was. I placed my other hand over it, cupping it; how tragic. Is the heart not the organ we long to know the most intimately? Recently, I had only come to know mine. For so long I had presumed it weak, feeble even, but now, I could not be more grateful for its enduring strength. As a woman, I had always been told to protect my heart, that it could so easily be tampered with and destroyed. Such warning only kept me from also truly experiencing the many wonderful things that only a heart could know. Though, yes, it endured many trials and tribulations, aches, and considerable burden, but also has it come to know many joys and successes. My heart, in conjunction with my mind, was truly the most capable of every inconceivable aspiration.

I blinked rapidly and strained my eyes. This shop was very well lit, and my tired eyes, which had become adjusted to settings with dim lighting, struggled to adjust to the brightness of this room. The light was fluorescent, and the white on the walls made it to appear as though it was brighter than it already was. The shelves held one more item, but not in a jar; instead, this item swam in a five-gallon fish tank. My head throbbed; it was a human brain. It explored the corners of the tank, floating from one corner to another aimlessly. An extraordinary thing it was, forever left to know that of the inside of four glass walls that held nothing at all but a victim of solitude. Certainly this mind had already lost its electric marvel, yet so easily though it captivated my own. What it had held it its possession, it was nothing other than a good gift, the first in its very own uniqueness. Yet, this good gift, though it was given in righteousness, perhaps in great creation too, was doomed to murder. A true tragedy. A mind such as this, a mind of any degree—to be lost, to be in any form contained.

I looked at this tank; my heart became troubled. Had I not, by finding this place, saved myself from such tragedy? Our minds, though intact and ostensibly functioning, can be lost so easily: lost to imagination, lost to daydreams, lost to hopelessness—a lost cause. Leaving you with the everlasting feeling that you had nowhere to go or no one to go to. Such a mentality had nearly captured me. The despair that became my livelihood, it robbed me of everything that I so desperately wanted; that mentality nearly stole my purpose of being. Here in this shop that smelled of death, I stared at what could very well be my deepest fear: the restraint of that which I deemed my most precious gift— my mind. The loss of something so exquisite, so very and absolutely priceless, would destroy me.

Labeled here too in red on the white tape was another word, another description made by this room, and it read "Able." I could not bear the sight any longer and turned away. My body was weak, and though this weakness did not reflect the state of my invigorated spirit, if I permitted it to, easily this exhaustion could steal from the other parts of me. I must stay strong in every aspect, in every regard to my persona. A new day, a new time, a new lesson; this too I shall overcome. Though my body was tense, nervous, and frail, I would never accept the limitations of my mind, soul, and spirit, for they were the fruits that would feed the many. The hungry, the sick, the dormant—they too can be awakened, healed, and mended, but not if they had already been made lost. I carried this thought and kept it in my heart, but now I must continue forward. There had not been a host made known for this room yet; there must be something that I was not seeing. I knew that there must be more than my tired eyes were able to see. So badly, I wanted to rest, but not here; first, I must meet this room's conditions. Then after, I could find my way home.

12

I LEFT BEHIND the shelves and their strange scenes of science. There were more people here—many more people. I was sure that if I could somehow connect and awaken with the frizzy blonde-haired woman, then maybe I would also be able to connect with another as well. My stomach still felt sick and queasy, which for what it had just seen was understandable. This smell, though, was horrid. There should be windows or air ducts for ventilation. The meat would not be very good for anything if it smelt this terribly. I kept my hand over my mouth, and my other hand covered my ear; I listened. The disembodied thoughts of everyone in this room hung above my head, and with sensitivity, I tried to discern one from the other but was unable to. I sighed. I wandered again through the crowd of people, moving myself to the front of the counter. I looked through the clear glass to take better note of the meats that sat for sale. Ordinary. Not at all did they look remotely appetizing. There was some variety; that I could not take away from it though. Ground beef, eye of steak, tongue of cow, the chop of a lamb, slices of pork, and many other types of grade and cuts.

I had never been one to indulge in protein; the smell of raw meat had always left my stomach unsettled, and its texture also left me without an appetite. This is what had everyone in line waiting so anxiously? The frizzy-haired blonde had said that she would wait longer than any else to be served, but to be served this meat? And how long had it even sat in this counter? I was more than sure that, by its appearance, it had already become rancid. Then such a thought was confirmed by the sight of a single fly probing the underside of a set of ribs; its antennas were perusing the surface, sucking in every available morsel of carnage. Disgusting. I had already become anxious, unsettled, and wanted to make progress already. There was soon going to be something that would test me, but I was unsure as to what. I walked unenthusiastically to another person that was waiting in front of the counter. This man was not waiting in line; he stood along those who crowded the counter. I bumped shoulders with the others who stood near him, but no one had noticed me yet, so I had no concern toward that of proper politeness.

I stood in front of a young man; he was slender with an athletic build and was lean and tall. His eyes were large like a doe and equally as dark. He was attractive and had a softness to his handsome features. This man, with a sharp jaw that wore the oncoming of a beard, was missing something. There was something that was lacking within him; it could be seen in his dark eyes, something that should be there, but it was not, and without it, he seemed incomplete. I took an awkward step around this man, angling my body away from his. Maybe this is not the man that I should speak to; easily I could find another here who did not have such effect on me. I turned to walk away, but I could not. He had, without a word, struck me, and though I knew it would do me no good, I approached him with the intention to unravel his desirable mystery.

He wore khaki pants, blue suede loafers, and a well-fitted button up. I stepped in directly in front of him, my body facing his, but still he did not see me. I stared into his dark eyes; they were the darkest of brown, as though they protected themselves from being read. He did as the blonde woman had done; he followed a routine of motions that were done in a mechanical sort of way, but his were not at all the same. He would turn his head around the room, as though he was looking for someone or something, then he would realize that it was not there. Then he would bow his head down and look back up, his eyes carrying even more sadness. I took a step forward to him and reached up closer to his face by standing on my tiptoes. He did not see me. With hesitance, I lifted my hand to place it on his temple.

When my fingers touched his light skin, he shook awake and stared deeply at me in my eyes. He furrowed his brow and spoke in a soft voice, "What are you doing?" I immediately regretted my decision and wanted to pull my arm away but did not; maybe he would answer the questions that I longed to know.

"I apologize. I just wanted to ask you a question."

His eyes darted away from me, and he retorted sourly, "I don't like being asked questions." His unwillingness to interact with me only stimulated my attempt to get that which I wanted: answers.

With a forceful tone of voice, I continued, "If I were to let you ask me a question, and I were to give you an answer that pleased you, would you then allow me to ask a question that, in turn, the answer would please me?"

He looked back down into my eyes and spoke, "Only if I am willing to answer will I. Go ahead, ask me what you want to know."

I pursed my lips and queried, "What are you waiting for?" He flared his nostrils and became noticeably agitated. I intervened, "Does that question not suit you?"

He looked down on me and said no.

"And why is that?"

He stood taller, adjusted his body, and placed his hands in his pockets. He turned to the left and said, "Because I do not know the answer to that question."

"You are telling me that you have been waiting but do not know what you wait for?" "Yes."

"Do you know what you want?"

"Of course I know what I want." He stared toward the counter and fell into silence. I did not urge him to answer; I simply waited for him to come to terms with his own thoughts. Then he spoke, digging his hands further into his pockets, "I know what I don't want. I know that much. Is that not more than what many other people know?"

His eyes looked lost, and I fell into the sorrow they evoked. With tenderness, I answered, "It is, that is much more than what many people would be willing to admit. Maybe that is what you are waiting for then: revelation of your true purpose."

"It is my turn now. I answered your question, now you have to answer mine." He looked sternly at me, as though I made him uncomfortable. "Why are you here speaking to me when you know, in your heart, that you should be accomplishing something of more importance elsewhere?"

I paused for a moment, insulted. I could not read him, but this man could read me. I thought about the many things that I had thought when first seeing him. Though he was physically handsome, I knew that he was more than that; this man had depth, but it was controlled by sadness. He waited for my answer. I ran my hand that sat on the temple of his head down his arm and held his hand.

He shuddered at my touch, as though he had never been touched in compassion before. His mouth almost turned into a snarl, but then he softened his lips and breathed in and out loudly.

I closed my eyes and composed myself. "The reason I stand here before you as a stranger is because you called me here."

He pulled away from my touch but did not let go of my hand. "I did no such thing. I do not want this, any of it; I just want to be given what is mine and to have nothing more taken away from me."

"I do not want to take anything from you. I want to give you something of importance; a message."

"A message? What message. I have not asked anyone for anything. I only want what was taken from me to be returned. That is all I want." His eyes were the saddest that I had seen yet. Filled with sorrow and loss, void of something that each human needed to be made whole.

I squeezed his hand and urged, "I do not know what it is that you have lost, but I am sure that this life will return it to you."

He said nothing at all; he just stared at the counter with longing and misery. "What has been taken from me cannot be returned, it is now forever lost, and so too am I." I empathized with this man.

I did not know what he looked at behind the counter. The butcher still paced behind it but did not use his knife to work. He seemed just as anxious as everyone else had. The murmur of the disembodied thoughts grew potently louder. I searched the room but did not see anything stirring. The murmur became louder.

"The message." I turned to him with a puzzled expression; he asked again, "What was the message you said you had?"

I swallowed hard, and with a cautious tongue I spoke, "You are worthy."

He closed his eyes, and they stayed closed for a long time, then finally he opened them and said, "Not by my own standards, this is what I for wait for—for the day that I am. You must go now. I thank you, but you must go. It will happen again. That which stole my first love will steal away every love to come. Go. Watch your step." He released my hand, and that was that. He returned to his monotony, looking for something that he had lost, knowing that he would never find it again.

I watched him for a moment more with deep sadness in my heart. I ached for him to find that which I had come to find. I did what I could; I gave him the message of my heart. One day, perhaps when he has come to terms with his great loss, he could come to believe such a message. I turned away from him. He reminded me very much of the man in the atrium who wore the green pants. They had the same type of sadness in their eyes. Though this man in the shop carried less anger. I wondered if the man from the atrium would be doomed to exist there, left to never truly know that tremendous beauty and hope that surrounded him. He, though, after he had seen me cough my soul's seed from my throat, refused to look at me again. I thought about the difference between these two men. They both had surmountable terms of growth to endure, both trapped by an unknown factor that they wished not to reveal but carry upon their own shoulders. This dark-eyed man, though, he acknowledged that he must undergo certain change before he could move on from the loss that visibly caused him much suffering. Perhaps I would never truly know the reasons. I did what I could to both; I gave the message that sat on my heart. With hope, I would move forward in faith that the seeds that I plant would be sown.

The crowd had become more anxious; the murmur grew louder but also vaguely more understandable. I tried to distinguish one thought from another, but as I came close, another would raise in volume and derail my train of thought. I looked at the crowd of people; everyone was only attentive to that of their own best interest. The two that I had spoken to were both adamant in receiving something that they believed to be theirs. It could not possibly be the meat behind the counter; certainly it must be something more. I felt a throbbing in my left hand and realized that I was still tightly gripping the number that I had pulled when first entering the shop; it was most assuredly crumpled by this time and had not yet come to serve an obvious purpose. I closed my fist tighter. What is it that I am to learn? And why had the host not come meet me yet? A shiver ran from my head to my bare feet, and I made an audible shudder.

There was an elderly lady standing in line in the third row. She seemed cordial, polite—much different than those that I had already interacted with. I stood next to her in her lavender cardigan; how badly I wanted it for myself. I felt the bottom of my nightdress for my raw diamond, and it was still knotted tightly within the fabric of my dress. Perhaps I could speak to one more person. If there was not a clear answer, then perhaps this might not even be a room at all but a waiting station. I turned back to look at the way I had come in, and it was there, still available as an option. This reassured me, for I had gotten nearly nothing from this room at all. Where was the host? I stood next to the elderly lady, and she smelled of lilac perfume. She carried a small white purse with daintily embroidered flowers on the rim. I reached my hand to her forearm. She awoke with a shake and quickly rubbed underneath her eye. She turned to me and smiled. "Sweetie, please wait your turn in line." My turn? Perplexed, I looked toward the counter and the one person standing ahead of her in the line. No one had received anything throughout the duration of my time spent it this shop. Not one person came in, not one out; nor had anyone been served anything whatsoever.

With frustration, I pleaded, "What is everyone waiting for?" Eagerly I stared at this woman with frantic eyes. My blood boiled. She smiled, and her smile mocked me. "Sweetie, it is best that you wait your turn, or you might regret it." That old crow! I was merely asking her a straightforward question, and now she belittled me and, furthermore, threatened me. Nothing at all was happening. The lines did not move; the meat sat there unpackaged and unserved. I was becoming maddeningly upset, and I could not keep the frustration from my voice, "I am not in line!" I yelled at this woman at the top of my voice and continued on, "That meat is rancid; it is decayed! Why on earth do you stand here waiting mindlessly for something so utterly stomach-churning? What is wrong with everyone? Answer me!" The murmur of the crowd roared loudly above my head. My anger was beyond that of control. I breathed in and out loudly. This old woman smiled at me with gum and teeth and said, "Were you not warned to watch your step? I told you, sweetie."

I could now hear the thoughts of the crowd. "Tasty. New. Long last." I tore my hand away from the woman and ran to the back of the room. Everyone who had had their attention so attentively toward the counter now stared at me. My stomach churned—what were they looking at? No, it couldn't be. The thoughts in the room became louder. The voices yelled and screamed proclamations of violence, loss, greed and, hunger. I wanted to scream, to run out of the door. These people, they intended to—and then, without warning, a man that was standing in line violently attacked another who had not been. They tore at one another in ways unimaginable; there was no humanity left at all. They fought and now rolled upon the floor, the crowd staring and cheering. Their thoughts were screaming death and gore. "Yes, survival is meant only for the victorious! Give me my share, I want what belongs to me!" The men struggled on the floor. The crowd stood motionless; their bodies did not react to what was happening, but their thoughts delighted in the scene. Their thought had become audible in a way that I could understand, although I wish I could not. In the air, their thoughts united and chanted in unison a horrible song, "Our eyes bear witness to crimes unanswered; the answers lie dormant in questions unasked, we blame one another and carry blades in our hands." Verse 1. "Our eyes bear witness to crimes unanswered, our heads lay to rest on sheets blood spattered." Verse 2. And then, with a ferocious crash, the man who stood out of line crushed the skull of the man who did against the white tile floor. Two, four, six.

I could not stomach the sight. He lay there, mauled and dead on the ground. Everyone turned their bodies and resumed the positions that they had previously had, and the murmur fell to a silent, disembodied whisper once again. The butcher came out from behind the counter and stood looking down over the mutilated body. He bent over and lifted the man from underneath his arms, dragging his body to where he had paced all this time and into the room that had no door. And as he drug the man, there was a trail of blood that was left, staining the white tile floor. I was nauseous. My mind could not process all that I had just seen. Then my stomach dropped; they had seen me, watched me intently previous to the attack, and then—how easily that attack could have been done unto me. I wanted to throw up, but there was nothing in my stomach, just bile and sickness. I stood there at the back of the shop, shaking. Watch your step. Watch your step. Watch your step. Then I heard the butcher's knife come down forcefully on the chopping block; he was preparing the latest kill. My eyes rolled behind my head, my stomach sunk, and I nearly fainted. This place was not at all what I expected. I thought that I would be guided, that a host would come to direct me, but no one came. Had I not been led to this place? Perhaps I was never intended to enter this room of death and slaughter.

I kept my eyes closed, but the smell—I could not escape the smell of freshly spilled blood. I wanted to weep—no.

Such would not be a demonstration of strength. Still, after all this, I did not know what this crowd waited for. I stood with slumped shoulders; how could any of this be? I turned to look at the shelves that carried the jars of organs; soon they would have additional company. Then there was a timid tap on my shoulder. "Did you pull a number?" I bolted away from this gesture in repugnance, nearly losing my balance and falling to the floor. I caught myself and stepped away from this man. I stared at him with wide eyes; after what I had just seen, after I had nearly slipped into their clutches, I must watch my step. This man did not seem intimidating at all; he had the appearance of a kind soul. Tall, with bent shoulders, dirty gray pants, and a balding head.

"No, no, no, no, no, no!" he repeated. "Do not worry! Oh, I did not mean to scare you. Sorry." He adjusted the horn-rimmed glasses that sat on his nose that were much too big for his face. He was sweaty, greasy, and smelled of body odor, almost as though his skin had absorbed the smell of the rancid meat. He adjusted his tie, which again was not proportioned properly to reflect his towering stature. It was quite funny actually; his voice was high-pitched and mousey, which was not at all what you would expect from a man of his giant stature. "They've made a mess, another mess. They will never learn." He thundered to the area where the fight had broken out, bent a knee to the floor, and complained, "Do you see this? Do you see what

I must deal with? Day in and day out. When will I rest?" He hacked a large, throaty wad of phlegm and spat it on the floor, then he pulled out a large white handkerchief and began to clean the trail of blood that had been left on the tile. He sighed heavily, "They will never learn. Never!" He huffed and puffed; his body seemed to ache, perhaps his frame could not support all the weight that he carried. His arms were so long that two extensions had nearly cleaned the entire trail.

He put his hand on his knee and forced his body up with a cringe and a moan made in pain. "Aye! This is getting old already; I'm getting old already." He trod toward me with large, lurching steps and then came to me and asked, "Are you well?" What a question that was indeed, the most spectacular question I might have been asked throughout this entire journey. There was a grand gesture in such a simple question.

"I have been significantly better," I said while stroking my arm to calm my nerves that were still petrified frozen.

He rolled his eyes and dramatically swept his arm to his forehead, "As have I! It has been dreadful here, just terrible." He spoke with such a casual tone of voice, like he always had visitors. This man, he must be this room's host; why had it taken so long for him to come to my side?

13

———⟡———

THE GIANT MAN—A giant I sincerely thought he was—dragged his great body around the shop. He must have stood at the height of at least eleven feet; though I had never seen anything like him, I did not have any worry when I was in his presence. Waving his mammoth hands around in fuss, he walked around the room, adjusting the people in the crowd as though they were mannequins. It was quite a sight to behold. When he would place his hands on the people, they would not speak or move. I went to where this man was working, rearranging the people in the shop. I approached him, and with a caring voice he squeaked, "Careful, little bug, careful; watch your step." I looked at the ground, but it was still the solid white tile that had covered the floor; there was nothing there. With caution, though I did not know why exactly I was asked to exercise it, I walked closer to this kindly giant.

"Little bug, that is refreshing. Do you call me that because I am so small and you are quite large?" I laughed, and he said, "No, I call you little bug because you can easily be squished like a little bug can be." I swallowed hard and tensed my body. "Oh no, little bug, I will not hurt you. Never, I would not squish you, at least, not on purpose."

I exhaled and continued the odd conversation. "So then I am to feel comfortable around you, is that what you wish?"

He smiled in an excited, dopey way and exclaimed in his mouse voice, "Why, yes; that would make me quite happy, oh yes. But, little bug, be careful with these; they bite." He nonchalantly picked up the man who I had found very handsome and placed him back in line. He was arranging the people who had crowded the counter back into neat rows of three. He did it so casually, as though it was part of his routine. Yet, this man, his stature was so large—how could I have not seen him in the shop before?

I again approached the giant so I would be standing next to him, so that I could have a closer view as to what was happening in regards to the people he was arranging. "If you are to call me little bug, then what is it that I should call you? I could call you giant."

He looked down on me and said, "No, do not call me giant. That is not my name; my name is Lou, call me Lou."

Lou, the giant who I had not noticed in the butcher's shop after spending so much time in it. "Lou, I like that.

Little bug and Lou." For some reason, even despite the tragedy I had just seen, I was in a very blissful and pleasant mood. "Lou, can I ask you some questions?"

"Yes, yes, go ahead but be careful." Lou was insistent that I heed caution in everything I did. If I were to sweep my arm to brush my hair out of my face, he would cringe and make faces of visible pain.

"I do not know where to begin, per se." I had seen so much, that there was no clear beginning, middle, or end.

Lou interrupted and, pronouncing every syllable with great preciseness and length, offered, "Then let me begin. You are not a very good listener. Did you not see all of the warnings that were outside of the door? Did you not see these people are missing something in their hearts? They are broken." He picked up a lady and set her down in the first line. "They are bad, they do not listen either. I place them neatly into lines every day, all the time, but they always do what they please. They want to be fed first." I listened to Lou, and he spoke in frustration, throwing his large hands up in the air then picking up another person and placing them into a line of his choosing. Lou went on, "Did you see them attack one another? They do that all the time. I am always having to clean up their messes. It's getting old now that I know how they really are."

I began to understand everything that I had seen, though not in the measures that I knew were needed. As my hands braided my loose hair, I retorted, "So then these people are like me—human."

"Yes, bug, they are human like you are."

"Do you collect humans?"

"Bug, I do not collect humans. I wish they would stop coming here, they always make such a mess."

"Do humans wander into this shop often?"

Lou picked up the blonde woman with the frizzy hair and held her in his giant hand; he licked his thumb and brushed it against her hair like she was a doll. "I do not like this one; she bites very hard. She will not be here much longer." He placed her last in the third line. "Humans wander in here all the time every day. They leave just as often as well, but some, like these, just can't seem to learn." I looked around at the many faces in the room. Everyone was different, but differences aside, they were stuck in the same room, and no one seemed to know for how long and or for what reason.

I found it ironic that again, the thing that people first lost when they could not identify with a personal fault was their voice. Just as it was in the atrium, it was parallel here in the butcher's shop and to those three people who I had spoken to earlier in the crowd: the frizzy haired blonde woman, the attractive dark-eyed man, and the elderly woman. Each of them spoke, but they did so with reluctance, and when I asked them what were questions of simplicity, they became frustrated, difficult, and distant. Perhaps here it was not the case of the loss of voice but the inability to know what was worth speaking. Each of them seemed to revel on a particular cause. The frizzy-haired blonde woman was more so concerned about obtaining that which she believed belonged to her; she did not mention what such an object was, then she asked if I intended to serve her. Such a question could only lead one to believe that she did not want simply any one thing but, instead, wanted everything. This was one reason I might have disliked her and her reason for disliking me; she knew that I would not be an individual who would bend at the knee, and I knew that she was not someone who I would wish to have further association with.

And the attractive dark-eyed man—he had something special, something beautiful to offer, but he could not overcome the loss of something so precious that had been taken from him some time ago. He had lost his first love, the love that brought light into his eyes, and without it, he knew not which direction to go. This I understood; the pain of losing a most loved one is nearly unbearable. The ache that you are left with endures an entire lifetime. Even worse, the amount of reflection made in regard to the "what if" physically hurts to know that life could be all the more if such a love had not been lost. He, though, knowing what was missing from his life, could not allow himself to move forward; in his lifetime, though opportunity might present itself on more than one occasion, he would believe himself to be unworthy of a thing as wonderful as love in fear that it would too be stolen from him in an untimely fashion.

The elderly lady, she simply did not want to be made a fool of and therefore treated others as though they were instead. She suffered from insecurity, a common human factor that could detrimentally affect an individual for an entire lifetime if they did not choose to actively fight such factors every day. Lou was correct in saying that humans never learn, for in some cases, we do not. It is not that we strive to be ignorant but more so that we fail to be wise. We are a stubborn sort, and though landslides may cripple us, we refuse to be kept from the path that we have set for ourselves. Furthermore, when it comes to be that that path we so passionately wish to pursue has been denied to us, rather than choosing another, we instead deny ourselves. This, again, is very human. In reference to everything that I have learned in this exploration of self, it cannot be denied that to come to terms with that of doubt and fear is the most crucial. To rid yourself of doubt and of fear is to eliminate like factors as well. Anxiety, insecurities, the assumption that you are not worthy of your heart's most-desired visions—these aspects may seem small until they cause you great struggle.

Lou was still arranging the people into neat lines; he would hum a tune and adjust their clothing or fix their hair. "So then, earlier, when I was wandering around the shop, I had looked everywhere, but you were nowhere. Where were you? You are so large, how was it that I missed you?"

He began to count the people that he set in line to see how many he had now and answered, "That is simple. You had not brought me into the room yet." I had no such control, unless—Fé did say, when we spoke at the luminescent mirror, that I was the one who decided how long I would be in each place. Is Lou now confirming what she had said?

This moment was opportune. With haste I asked, "Then where were you before I called you in?" He looked at me, and his horn-rimmed glasses slipped down his nose. With his great finger he pushed them back into place; he answered in a tone of voice that made me feel like he did not exactly understand the question, "Well, I was doing what you are doing now." With concern, he looked at me and continued, "Are you not undergoing a process of self-discovery in the most peculiar of ways, bug?" I stared at him in return with my mouth agape. It was true, I was, but what did my journey have in common with that of his absence from this room?

I began to walk between the rows that Lou had set up and noticed something that did not sit very well with me. "Lou, this third row of people. You said that the frizzy haired blonde woman would not be here much longer, is that why she stands last in line?"

"Yes. She always bites. I have been kind to her, but she always bites me."

"I do not hear you speaking to them when you are placing them in order; how then have you shown her kindness?"

"Well, bug, I am not human. I am not like you, so my ways will not be the same as your ways."

"Then how are you speaking to me in a way that I can understand?"

"Because you have made it that we could." Again, he insinuated that I had control over the many variables of this place. I looked to the first row of people, and the dark-eyed man stood third in line. "If the third line means that are not yet close to meeting the conditions of the room, then does that mean that the first row is a step closer to reaching home?"

"Yes." This, again, caused unsettlement.

I walked to the first row and stood next to the attractive young man. "Lou, what force empowers you to make these decisions?"

He looked at me again with deep concern. "How many rooms have you visited?" he asked. Of what alarm was this to him?

"I have technically been to two places: both the atrium and the stone cavern."

"All right, yes, and how did you come to reach them?"

"I came by the stairs of my very own home. Then I happened upon a warehouse with dilapidated factory machinery, but no one was there—well, except for him."

"Him, regarding the great darkness of your life."

How did Lou come to know this name? I approached him, and with anger, I scolded, "How do you know of him? I have not told you anything at all in regards to him!"

Lou pulled the handkerchief that he had used to clean away the previously shed blood from his pants pocket, used it to clean the top of his balding head, and politely responded although I spoke in a vulgar tone, "You asked earlier how I was able to be kind although I did not speak to these people; did you hear the disembodied thoughts that hung in the air earlier? You are human, bug; your thoughts and your inner feelings were also part of that which was incomprehensible to your ears but completely understandable to mine."

I was embarrassed. I had never spoken to anyone about the darkness that I had seen; it had always been kept as a most personal secret. I did not want to be made to look as though I did not have control of myself or of my life, yet, in reality, until now, I never did. "Even now, are you able to hear all that is in my mind?"

"Yes, bug."

"Where will you put me?"

He looked around at all the people who, to him, must have looked very small, myself included. He smiled warmly, and although his teeth were not particularly pleasant to the eye, I was solaced. "Did you pull a number?" he asked with a sensitive voice. I had forgotten that in my clenched fist was the slip of paper that I had been carrying with me all this time.

"I did, but I have yet to look at it." What would this paper reveal to him that he could not have taken from my thoughts? If he wished to know who I was, could he not just listen to that of my mind?

I clenched my fist harder. I did not want this paper to determine whether I did or did not move forward; that was only for me to determine. It was not even the host who had such power, not even Lou, who stood towering over these people, arranging them by their capabilities. No, I refused to be held from moving forward. I wanted to go home. I intended to make great change. "Must I look at what I pulled?" Lou turned to listen to the knife that still hit loudly against the chopping block. "Not yet, bug. First, I would like you to answer a question for me. Can you do me that favor?" The knife hit forcefully, and flashes of what had happened came across my mind. Murder.

I looked up to Lou, "Of course, ask me whatever you wish to know."

"All right, bug, this is my question to you. If a man stands in line and another does not, then who is on the chopping block?" He must be referring to that which had taken place. It was the man who was in line that charged the man who stood out of line, but it was the man who stood out of line that was victorious.

Again, the knife viciously cut against the fresh flesh of man. An answer to such a question is gravely dependent on the situation and the perspective of each side. How can I doom a man to death based solely upon where he stands? Whether if he stands on stone or sand, he is man all the same. If he picks up a pen with his left or right hand, it is of no matter; he is a man. When these men broke into their ravenous frenzy, there had been no sign that pointed to violence nor were there weapons or a declaration of war. I closed my eyes and tried to listen to the drone of disembodied thoughts that were in the air, but still I could not hear them. I looked up to Lou and in turn asked, "You hear that which is in the air, yes?"

"Yes."

"Then this shall be my answer to you: These words, to your ears, are clear and concise, yet when I hear them, they sound like multiple people trying to find their path in a world that they do not understand. As to who is in the wrong, it is not my duty to point a condemning finger. My question, a question that I think would be more proper, would be this: did each man, whether in line or out of it, fight knowing that he was laying down his life? If life is on the line, then so is that matter that initiated such a brawl as well, is it not?"

Lou raised his arm, rubbed the top of his head in a sloth-like manner, and responded, "If a man is asked to lay down his life, then this man, if of a sound mind, would reevaluate that which he is fighting for. So yes, bug."

"Good, I am glad that we are able to agree on that matter because then that matter brings us to this point. This shop, I am assuming, highlights the worries of man. These individuals are aware of their shortcomings and, in self-defense, initiate their innate human instinct of preservation."

These people, they did not want to fight or to begin to tear one another apart out of hate or pastime; they simply wanted to survive and defend their platform for a new beginning. Of course they waited long enough, and they would wait much longer too—as long as was needed. I would as well; I have and will continue to. I understood why they wished to be served; had they not already lost so much? This shop—it was that which makes a man new.

"Lou, to be made anew, you need not new flesh, but only the renewal of that which has already been given to you."

He, at this point, was cleaning the top of the silver aluminum counter of the deli that stored the meat. Did people truly think that a new body meant a new beginning? We are given our physicality at birth; it is thus our responsibility to maintain ourselves. So often we take what we are given for granted. Bags sit dark underneath our eyes, wrinkles dug by worry appear upon our foreheads, and calluses emerge upon our tender palms; such is age but also abuse. The shelves in the back of the shop—the labels could not have been written with more truth. The eyes that sit in our heads, we pray that they have twenty-twenty vision not only in terms of sight, but also in terms of ambition. We want to know the destination we seek and when we will arrive, yet each step we take in hesitation leads us further away. If we know not where we go, then how shall we come to reach such a destination, and although happenchance does vaguely affect the time in which we will spend in the unknown, do we not control the path that we venture?

To the heart labeled distant, do not listen to the many who speak ill of your tenderness toward the hands that have touched your life. Coldheartedness is not a feature of the gentle, and the gentle have been scabbed and scarred by those who have forfeited such a kindness. You need not a new heart but a new appreciation of self. Look to yourself and your neighbor; there is remarkable worth, a heart that knows no love is not a heart at all. Is it not a muscle? And must not a muscle be exercised? To push away a hand that reaches out to you in compassion is not an act of love but an act made with the intention of disconnect. To you I ask: Will you not offer opportunity to the one who you have sent away time and time again, who has returned to you asking for no more than a chance at your heart? Be kind, for the many times that you have sent them away with rejection on your tongue, you, in turn, do to them as you have done to yourself: turning that which is beautiful into a thing of denunciation. Want for nothing, not from him nor from her; be of carefree design. Hearts anew are not grown from maddening heartache but form from sudden revelation. Your heart knows many loves but none at all. Be soft; love cannot be forced, only illuminated.

We are the hand that poisons our own well-being. It is not the mug that forces itself upon our dry lips but the hand that raises it. Many men have drank themselves to death and very few to greatness. Let me ask you this: If you have not had a drop of water and dust sits in your mouth, would it be wise to labor under the basking sun? You will become burned and will voice frustration; would you not claim thirst? And when offered water, why must you continuously reject it? Would it not quench your thirst? If you wish to labor and to do great work, then please, will you not take a sip of water, freely given, to restore your health and fulfill your physical need? To practice acceptance in an era of stubbornness is to spare your tongue the thorn and offer it the gift of merely a sip of healing water.

Your mind is able; it is your pride that is not. Lay it down; it is man who has taught us to fear and doubt. Of the many great losses to endure, would it not be the greatest loss of all to lose your mind and, ultimately, yourself? Be proud but not prideful; to those who parade their many artificial achievements, learn to be humble. For the humble are looked upon with both admiration and reverence. If you have everything that you could wish for, share it, give it away; what better a gift to share than that of your own most brilliant insight. Speak, for when you know it not, you are being heard and softening the hearts of those whose ears your words fall upon. Mind you, be wary of your tongue. If you do not give thought to that which you speak, then you are worse than war; do not take joy from others to fill the void that you have created within yourself. Your mind is the birthplace of many extraordinary things; great is our vice, and greater is our purpose.

The people that had crowded in this room that now stood in three separated and neat lines by Lou's hand, I believed that one day too they would be able to leave and find their way home. When they no longer did as they had always done, when routine was then acted in pleasure rather than in need or greed, then, yes, they can be with laughter, wearing crowns upon their lovely heads. This I too believed, that our tongues hold much power, and I want not evil to fall from my own. After witnessing everything that I had in this room, I decided that I would allow moments of weakness to instead transform into periods of reflection; only then can we be strong enough to stand without the weight of the world to bend us. For one day the earth shall cease, and today, that is all the encouragement I need.

I pulled my consciousness back from where it had run off to and directed my attention toward Lou; he was still cleaning and tidying up the shop although it, aside from the smell, was pleasant. "Lou, I am confident now in my ability to move forward from this place."

"Are you, bug? Do you know what lies ahead?"

"No, Lou. In all honesty, I do not know the many details that I am sure lie ahead, but that does not concern me in a troublesome way."

"Are you ready for anything, then, bug?"

"I believe that I am, yes."

And with that, Lou went to pull the attractive dark-eyed man from the original spot that he had placed him in: the first line in the third spot. He did the same with his opposite hand, picking up the frizzy blonde-haired woman from her spot: the third line in the fourth spot. He lifted them both up by their waists, crossed his arms, and placed each of them in one another's spots, completely changing their fates by switching the places that they had been set.

I became manic and ran toward the young man, stopping to look at the sadness that filled his doe eyes. With a loud voice I yelled, "Lou, put him back where he was! You are dooming him to lose his life if you leave him here. This is not where you had placed him. Fix this—fix this immediately!" Lou watched me with his giant eyes, but they did not look at me with concern; instead, he continued to go about resuming his miscellaneous tidying. I weaved between the lines of people who stood lifelessly, awaiting their fate, and stood in front of Lou. "Please, Lou, put him back where he was. He was more willing to admit his faults than she was!" I turned to look at the blonde woman who stood in line; she did not move from her previous heel-to-toe manner; she just stood there with the same facial expression of disdain that she wore when I had spoken to her earlier.

He moved them as though they had been chess pieces, like he was practicing some sort of winning strategy. I closed my eyes and forced my lungs to breathe in the rancid smell of decaying meat; this is what he wanted, for me to become bothered. Always in these rooms were the hosts testing me in manners that were in many ways bizarre. If he wished to make a point, why could he just not ask me? He knew the importance that this young man represented in my life, though I knew him not. How dare he use his ability to understand that which I did not even speak to him; he invaded my mind and broke the barrier of language. I clenched my fist hard; I had to calm down. He was inside my mind listening to my most personal thoughts.

Finally, I was able to speak in an even tone; thinking out loud, I spoke, "It was beyond comprehension how we could accept tragedy so easily and without a doubt but reject one another without reason." Lou lent me his attention and looked down on me from above his tipped, framed glasses. I went on. "I do not understand it at all."

He began to pick underneath his fingernail and regarded me. "You understand to some degree, do you not, bug?" I had won him over to conversation. He licked his thumb and tried to tame the frizzy hair on the head of the blonde woman.

"I thought that you said that you did not like that woman?"

He continued doing what he was and said, "No, she bites hard."

"Then way did you move her to the front and him to the back?"

"Well, bug, you said that you felt as though you were prepared for whatever was to come; I just wanted to show you that you are not." I gasped and pulled my head back.

"You would put his life on the line to teach me a lesson?"

"Did you learn something, then, bug?" This great but gentle giant taught me a lesson indeed. My heart raced, and I wanted nearly nothing more but for him to put the young man back in the spot that he was in.

I swallowed my pride and put aside the games that I had begun to play; I sulked and said, "Love is not to be learned but to be demonstrated. I would cut the tongue from my own mouth if my presence alone could speak the volumes that my heart had not the vocabulary to confess. Unsure legs will always run to strangers and fall on to weak knees, begging for the acceptance that they deny themselves."

"Bug, yes, good job! But there is more."

"More?"

"Little bug, you insist on entertaining a fabrication of a man. Don't you see that you are inviting your own heartache? He is trapped within his own skin; must you have him reject your affections to realize this? He sent you away. You are worthy of a love that revitalizes, not exhausts. Put all other expectations to rest." Lou looked at me with softness. Then he extended his arms out, grabbing both the blonde and the young man again by the waists, and put them back into the spots that they had been in originally. "I have heard that it can be a very sad thing to be human, bug. Do not worry. You will be found. He will be too."

I could not bring myself to say anything at all, for my heart did not have the words. I was happy; at least now he would have a chance.

"Bug," chimed Lou.

I did not pull my eyes away from the young man and replied, "Yes, Lou?"

"You pulled a number; it is time that you read it. Read it out loud, bug." I lifted my clenched fist up to my chest, then out, and opened up my hand. Using both hands, I uncrumpled the piece of paper and saw my number. Two hundred forty-six. My stomach dropped, and I was once again reminded of the fear and doubt that I still had to run from, even in this place. Lou waited for me to speak, his attentive ear already knowing what it would hear. "Two hundred and forty-six," I retorted.

"Yes, bug, and what does that mean to you? I know that you say it often." I did say it often—more often than I wish I had.

14

IN BOLD RED the number 246 was written on this
white slip of paper in the same manner exactly as how
those mason jars containing the vital organs had been
labeled by that which had hindered them. Again I had been
made vulnerable by that which limited by ability to become
all that I could be. I thought of Fé, how I had disappointed
her and then come to redeem myself. Could I also not be
able to redeem myself here in this situation as well? I took
a deep sigh and quickly exhaled; my stomach was empty,
and I did not like the way the scent of carcass lingered in
my lungs. The butcher that had paced behind the counter
still cut away; his sharp chopping knife would hit the block,
tearing away at what remained of that man who had been
mauled. There was a clicking of glassware, and out from
the room from behind the counter came the butcher. In
his hands he carried jars, and on those jars there was white

tape; in them floated the organs whose time had just been recently cut short.

Lou grabbed the jars and pulled a red marker out from his pant pockets; he lunged to the shelves in the back of the room with a sluggish, heavy foot. He scribbled words onto the tape, and then he carefully placed the jars on the shelves alongside the others. I knew that this would happen, and I was sad that it had. I looked down again to my number. Yes, this number did carry important significance to me even though I wish it did not. Any time—every time—fear or doubt would overwhelm me, I would count in even numbers to try and keep me calm. I had always been a fearful child—afraid of the dark, of heights, of being home alone. If I wanted to be brave, to pretend that I was strong, I would count two, four, six. I would not run, I would walk, and I would not hold my breath; I would speak. I did my best to keep my steps confident to exercise faith, hope, and love.

I felt overwhelming sadness; such a confession caused me pain, not pain in a physical sense but in a way that made me reevaluate all that I had come to learn. I turned to Lou, this towering giant, and opined, "What if morning does not come?"

"Then we shall remain amongst our dreams, against the heartbeats of our most loved ones."

"And if we are alone?"

"No one is alone but by his own choosing." Lou had touched my heart with his simple words; how profound he was, yet, how could he not be? He had access to the many minds that he surrounded himself with, and though they all might not know it, each of them were worthy and offered a contribution of great significance. I stared at the jars that sat on the shelves, wondering what might be said of me when all had come to pass. Lou interrupted my frame of thought and conceded, "Look at what you've become, little bug. Some call it adaptation, evolution; they are merely surviving, and they call it life. You, little creation, were meant to defy all reasonable explanation." I could not help but break down at this moment; no tears fell from my eyes, but there was a fire in my soul. There was a fire in me, within me; greater it burned, with purpose and passion. This fire could not be taken away from me. I had been enlightened; they couldn't forcefully remove me from this place that had finally brought me solitude, where I had finally found peace after all these long years of agony. It had been as though my insides were set afire, yet no sensation of pain was present. There was no discomfort, no yearning to evade the flames that were presumably swallowing me whole. I had finally come to know my purpose and, even more, found passion in the idea of protecting it and seeing such purpose through. This purpose was the fire in me. Always would it be mine, and no one else would be able to steal it away from me.

Passion consumed my entirety, and I was thrilled to carry the message that sat on my heart; so willing was I. All I could do was warn those who stood in this room. I spoke in a sure voice and proclaimed, "How can I sit still, silent, when our existence is deteriorating? Crooked ceilings are collapsing, the weathered walls are painted bloodred—it's terribly worrisome. I cannot stand still! This world is crippled, weak, coughing up lies, and spitting up blood—choking. Listen to me: We are our own medicine. We are our own greatest hope!"

I looked to Lou; he smiled down at me and adjusted his glasses. He nodded his head in agreement and said, "Bug, though you are very small, I know that you will not allow yourself to be stepped on. Be careful, watch you step. And do not be fearful or doubtful; it is human to call out for help. I am proud to know you, bug. Go now. You must go while your heart is ready. Behind the counter there is an entrance; go through it. Watch your step, little bug."

Although I entered in sickness, I was able to meet this room's condition. I was moving forward with confident steps, the fire burning fearlessly without a doubt in my heart. My heart sang! Understand this. No misjudgment is so shameful that you must endure such terrible anguish. Brokenness is only brokenness if you allow it to remain untended. I am absolutely mad—mad for pain, mad for passion, and mad for purpose. My soiled lungs are filled with rancid air; they gasp and gain nothing, but still they are in hope for resurrection, for a life spent no longer recklessly burning borrowed time. It's sick, but I am not—not any longer. My hands are contaminated by the earth's scum, my knees coated in soot; the many countless people are searching so desperately. Some days I feel like I am nothing but swine wallowing in mud, filthy and forsaken, but every day I will choose life. I want to live every day with passion in my heart and with purpose on my tongue; the day that I do not is the day that I am dead.

Maybe what it is is that we have become comfortable; we have allowed ourselves to become bystanders, pedestrians, merely witnesses. We find no fault in ourselves or in our actions; we do not intend to find such fault. We have lived in ignorance, in pleasure, and in sadness. We cannot pinpoint the reason, and if it fell upon our laps, we would sweep it away, and obvious hope would be left disregarded. It is lovely and it is necessary to be raw. I've found comfort in my vulnerability. I'll find no pain now that I am becoming unphased toward that of fear and doubt. I will not simply survive; I will not crawl on hand and knee through mud and filth any longer. My lungs may breathe in this disgust of death and rancid decay, but no longer will I permit such toxins to sit within me. I will inhale, exhale, and breathe anew—always new.

With a wave of my hand I said good-bye to Lou; though he did speak as the other hosts had, he left me with much comfort and new hope. I knew where I needed to go. I looked at the faces of everyone standing in line, and to each of them I gave my love and best wishes. And to him I knew that one day, his heart would be softened, and he would come to believe the message that my heart had shared with him. I approached the butcher's counter; the smell of blood was strong and fresh. I swallowed hard and held my breath because I had just found that which filled my lungs with new hope and did not want the earth to come to taint it. I was now behind the butcher's counter, and I wished not to see what he was chopping—not at all. Both Fé and Lou had told me that I was somehow able to control the things that I came into contact with; if that was so, then I could also control that which I did not wish to see.

The knife, again, hit the chopping block again. With my tongue I spoke, for I knew that with it I could make great change, and softly I spoke into existence this thought: "I understand that there has been a tragedy. I have seen it once, and I do not wish to see it again." I took a step forward and did not hear the knife fall on to the block for a second time. I turned back once more; Lou was still fussing with the order of those who were not yet able to move forward. I looked to the handsome young man, and in his line he stood, unaware of what another was willing to do just for him. I looked at the entrance to this next room and took a confident step through it, and there was no mutilated body laying there. There was no butcher, no blood or gore. I was standing in a patch of forest, and shortly up ahead I could see what looked to be a corridor. With spirit I went forward; I had been reinforced, and now I was prepared.

This life had proven itself to be rather difficult; it had broken many hopes and dreams, yet my soul has been set on fervent fire. This life, though testing, has also greatly discouraged the doubt, fear, the sadness, and anger that had festered for so long in my heart. And although I walked through this forest alone and had some ache, I was comforted. I walked on what was a dirt trodden road; it had already been compacted and was solid against the bottom of my foot. There were trees with branches that hung low. Again my eyes had to adjust because the light was now dim. These trees did not have many leaves on them; instead, they were scattered alongside the low shrubbery alongside the beaten path. There was an open space on the left-hand side of the path, and with readiness I approached it. Just like the sign that had been shown to me in the stone cavern, here too was a message. It was illuminated in gold with lovely penmanship; I had nearly forgotten the warning that had been left for me in the stone cavern. It had warned me to pay attention to that which was around me and to respect the flame that would stand with me. I did not understand then what such a message had truly meant, but now, holding that fire of purpose and passion within me, I was prepared for what lay ahead. After all this time, I would be asked to face the great darkness of my past.

With a low voice I read aloud the message, and like this, it was read: "Tread quietly, whisper. Move forward more briskly. Avoid the branches, the thicket, the shade. Mud smeared across pale faces; the disease is spread. Taste it, spit it out; the tongue lashes in defiance. Run forward, wide deer eyes, into the wilderness, into the world. Perhaps it will feed you or you it. Run ahead, hopeful youth, declaration is near."

This overwhelming experience of realization of self has been nearly indescribable. I have tried so many times to put it into words, but my soul does not permit it. It yearns to taste the epiphanous escape ten times more then multiplied by three. If I continue in this unamendable state of ache, truly, neither earth or down below could comfort such inconsolable sorrow. I shed myself of doubt and of fear, of what had be to be sacrificed in order for me to move forward. Although my body should be cold, it was not, for the warmth in my spirit soothed me, and onward I went through this short patch of forest. The corridor was right up ahead. It was modern in design with gray on the walls, embellished by decorative displays of the colors black and white. I was glad that the carpeting was black, for if it had been white, my bare feet would have stained it. It smelled good, which was, for the sake of my lungs, a luxury.

There was a door visible at the end of the short corridor. Confidently I approached the shadowed line of the door and reached to open it.

A new room. It was carpeted in gray; the walls were gray and the ceiling as well—all gray. From the ceiling there was a low-hung chandelier, simple in appearance, but it was beautiful all the same. There was a wet bar along the left side of the room; the spirits were displayed in fine crystal with tumblers to match. On the other side of the room were three king-sized mirrors. Extravagant in proportion, each of them was displayed in the same silver frame. At the center of the room was the most gorgeous mahogany desk that I had ever laid my eyes upon; it was luxurious, with details made by the hand of the finest craftsmanship. There were chairs on each side. At the head of the desk there was a white high wingback chair; it was of imperial design, lovely and rich. On the other side of the desk was an extraordinarily simple wooden chair. I approached the desk and ran my fingers across its fine surface, perfectly shined and done so to suit royalty. I placed my hand on the white wingback and looked around; there was no one there. I sat on the chair and made myself comfortable. I had not sat down, at least not comfortably, for some time. I leaned back, crossing my legs and looking at the modern display of this room.

I had lifted myself out of the chair, wiping away any debris that I may have left. Still I did not see anyone. I walked toward the right wall, approaching the center mirror, and kept in mind to be wary of all the warnings that had been given to me. I looked at myself in the mirror. I stood straight with my shoulders rolled back; there was confidence, and seeing a characteristic that you had struggled so very much to obtain was reassuring to say the least. I thought of Fé, Za'ara, Lou, and even of Maelzer. Each of my hosts had served such inspiring purpose and led me to become the woman who I was now so happy to see in the mirror. The raw diamond still hung at the hem of my dress; I made a quick circle to see how I looked.

I did not look tired. My brown eyes still had faint gray shadows set beneath them, highlighting the exhaustion, but soon I would be able to rest. My lips still, and for the rest of my life, would have questions to ask of any willing ear. My eyes—my dark eyelashes were sure and confident; never had my vision allowed me to see more clearly. Health-wise, my condition had greatly improved and that of my heart; my heart was sure to endure, my character would continue to flourish, and my entirety was becoming stronger than imagination could have dreamt. I had used to think that my soul had been meant for another body, a body more able to hold it in place, but, no, I had been greatly mistaken. My petite frame was vessel enough for the undying flame that burned within me. I had always been so worried at the idea of losing myself to this earth that seemed to thrive on loss;

I did not desire to feed what had only stolen and starved those who had given it everything. Now, I could act as a beacon of light, and no longer would I simply witness the tragedies of the world.

I looked over to the right mirror then to the left one, and then frighteningly, I jumped aside in alarm. In the left mirror was a reflection of a man who stood with a dashing white smile in the room next to me. I jumped back; he found it quite amusing that his presence had startled me. I placed my hand over my heart, and I tugged my nightdress down; this fellow had a wandering eye and very little cordialness. He had fine blond hair on ivory skin; his eyes were like that of a star, as gray and as bright. He wore a well-fitted charcoal suit, and his style was much like that of the room; this must be its host. He walked toward me, then around, staring impolitely at me while he did so. His gray eyes darted up toward me, and with a cool laugh, he asked, "Did I frighten you?"

15

———— ❈ ————

I TOOK A step away from him and mimicked the circle that he was walking in; we measured one another as though we were competitors. This man found himself to be quite a catch; that sparkling smirk had not fallen off his face. I pulled my hair over to one side, responding to his arrogant demeanor; how badly I wished to be wearing something other than this unappealing nightdress or to at least have slippers of some sort. Watch your step; no matter how comforting the setting might be, my guard must stay up. I stood tall though; arrogance was not an attribute that caused me apprehension. Whatever this fellow had in store for me, I was prepared. We continued watching one another as we both walked in this circle; he had a particular manner of moving his body. It was eerie, yet in some form, I recognized it. He stared me square in the eyes, like he was observing me in a carnal way. The still voice that I learned to heed spoke warning, and I looked down to the ground to watch my step.

"Are you frightened? Perhaps I should have not snuck up on you in such a manner. I do beg your sincerest of apologies." I looked back up to him, and his bright smile flashed across his pale face once more. "I'm sorry, have I offended you in some way? Such was never my intention." He laughed heartily and then quickly stopped. "How rude of me, I haven't even offered you a drink; would you care for one?" Though he was not particularly bad-looking at all, I did not intend to become friendly with this man. He was untrustworthy; a sympathetic host I knew he would not turn out to be. There was a knot in my stomach, and my head began to ache; I watched him. He fiddled with the cuffs of his jacket and proceeded to remove it, looking up and asking me, "It is rather warm in here, is it not?" I stared at him with stern eyes; it was obvious that he enjoyed this banter, this game of cat and mouse. He knew that his presence made me uncomfortable, and it pleased him to some degree. He crossed underneath a shadow, lingering there for just a moment. He turned over his shoulder to look in my direction; the shadows engulfed half of his face, and his features were swallowed by darkness.

Revelation. That is how I recognized him. Two, four, six. I would need to keep caution; the game had never been played by these rules before. I closed my eyes, preparing myself for the onslaught that was soon to come. I must practice patience to avoid being victimized. I did not particularly like to be caught off guard; I had been before, but never again. I must not let him know that I was a step ahead. The fire in my heart burned vehemently. A wildfire within my soul and spirit, calming the madness that I now named passion. With a deep breath I lifted my hand to the back of my neck and stretched, leaving my hand over my forehead, absentmindedly acknowledging his presence. "Perhaps we could sit down; I have the coming on of a headache, and I just became rather dizzy." He walked toward me in effort to aid, but I did not let this monster touch me. I dodged his effort, and he turned to me with a severe brow. With false obliviousness I responded, "Oh, I am sorry, how blind of me; I nearly did not even see you coming in my direction." I did my best to wear a face of innocence, but a smirk curled on my lips nonetheless. He stood up, adjusting his white button down shirt.

"Hope can blind even the most focused of eyes," said the man in the charcoal gray suit, flashing his devilish smile at me.

A move well played, but no matter; it was my turn. I turned my hair over to the other side of my shoulder and took a step, turning away from him, and through the mirror, my eyes met his, and he smiled again. "And what do you know of hope?" I asked him with waning sharpness on my tongue.

He lurked around behind me and whispered behind my neck, "Don't you think I'm worthy of all the happiness of the world as well?" I pulled away from him in disgust and retreated toward the wooden chair. I sat down and did not look in his direction. "Oh, so is this how you're going to treat your dashing young host? I thought that you would prefer this body much more than the other?" He grinned menacingly at me; he confirmed my previous thought—this monster.

"It is not your body. Did you steal that as well? Isn't everything you own by that of thievery?"

He laughed harder diabolically. "Thief? I much prefer the term of cunning. Was there not a time that you were—what did you like to call that trick of yours?—ah, yes, clever! Was there not a time that you and I were so alike?"

I pushed back the wooden chair—no. I must stay cool just as he is, and twice as much. He came toward the desk and sat on its sturdy edge, staring at me for a moment; he leaned in closer, but I did not flinch my face. I kept my expression strong. He went around the desk and sat in the high wingback chair across from me, leaning back and crossed his leg over his knee. "Ah, yes, frustration; you wear it quite well. It has always been my favorite look on you. Certainly much better than this, how shall I say, nightgown? It leaves everything to the imagination and nothing for the eye; that's just selfish of you!" This monster, objectifying me! I adjusted myself in the uncomfortable wooden chair; sweeping my hair again in front of my shoulder. I knew that he wished to make me uneasy in the skin that was my own; I shall not let him, not ever again. He sat smugly on the white chair and enthusiastically continued, "I once knew a girl. You might have known her as well; she was a pretty little thing: vulnerable, doubtful, filled with fear—ah, yes, she was truly my favorite. She ran far away and left herself behind. Night after night and throughout the duration of her days she writhed in depression, calling out to nothing, wishing that it would call back. It did many a time; what it was I will leave to your discretion, but it did return her call. I simply intercepted it. I prefer pretty, sad little girls, and she, she had much potential. It would have hurt me greatly to see such a thing bloom."

The color that had swept my cheeks fell away and choked me. Two, four, six. The bloom of my soul's seed would endure, and so too would I. Foregone ache. How well he did know me? But then again, it had been many years that we had been together. He rested his elbow on the mahogany desk, leaned forward, and rested his chin upon his fist. "What is it? Do I not make you happy anymore? You have always been my favorite brunette—well, when you were wearing clothing other than that drab!" He leaned back and looked at his fingers. He exaggeratingly sighed and rolled his eyes. "You are no fun! This change, it does not suit you. You are not that which you have come to convince yourself that you are! As entertaining as it is, I would like you to return to that which you were, to that which you will always be. Had I not been the voice to whisper sweet lullabies into your ear when you thought that no one heard? Listen to me, have I not always made you happy?"

He made me cringe; how could I have been his puppet for so long? The most devastating part was that every word he spoke, in this one thing, was the truth. I had been all that and more. In this place, never had I been asked to lean on any other source but myself. I had not been able for so long, and after all this, I found that so easily I could stand on my own. Those things that enabled me to do so, they had been missing my entire life, and now they could not be taken away from me, not as long as I watched my step. I composed myself and then replied, "I do not agree. To place your happiness in another is to ensure inevitable sadness."

"Oh. This is quite the conversation for the two of us to be having, isn't it? I am quite pleased that you have been able to find such temporary happiness; between you and me, you had always been so forlorn. The reason why is still such a mystery to this very day. It will be quite refreshing to take this that you think is yours away." He twisted his body in delight; games, yes, he had always been very good at them. At first I had believed that it was him who had called me into this place, but that was not the case; truth be told, he had not been able to drown away that omniscient presence that called me here. He is frantic; though he dare not reveal such truth to me, I would pull it out of him. Of that I had no concern.

With a tense lip I looked him in his stardust eyes and said this, "I wish you well. I am not as I was before. Your whispers will not reach my heart, and though my ear may hear you, it will not listen." Yes, there. I could not listen to his lies any longer; though he spoke with elegance and familiarity, he did not and never will have best my intent at heart. Monsters do not have hearts; they had been forfeited to the darkness from which they came. With purpose and warning, to him I spoke, "Do not attempt to console me with tender words of comfort; such kindness only has temporary effect. Instead, I will simply, and confidently, claim that which my soul longs for. Faith is the foundation which enables action. Only then can peace be attained, and only then will it be mine eternally."

He lifted his eyebrows, and the fun that he had seemed to be having was quite gone now. "Oh, are you a poet now?"

"I can now be anything that my heart desires, no thanks to you. I received my answers, and they are grand."

He waved his hand around in circle near his ear, as though he insinuated that I was talking much more than he liked. He scoffed then mockingly replied back in the tone that I had just used, "What a shame to live in fear of darkness, for with gentle arms, he cradles the night sky glittered with the stars we find ourselves begging for answers." He seemed rather proud of himself; he was always glad to poke fun at that which was of importance to the hearts of those he tormented.

I admitted I was relieved that he was in this form rather than the one that I had refused to look at when in the alleyway. I knew that this time, the sight of him would not cause me such great irascibility. Without allowing his attitude, or presence, to be of great bother, I casually cooed, "How sad it must be for the fallen to roam this earth, coaxing lies into vulnerable ears when they themselves know the truth."

This visibly irritated him, and he shifted himself into a less lax sitting position. "This has been quite fun, but it is now time to discuss the business at hand." He drew out, from a drawer in the desk, some sheets with black ink typed on them. He held out the stack of sheets and tapped them twice on the desk in a manner of organization. He laid them down on the table and turned them to me, sliding them to me. From the same drawer he pulled a pen as well and placed it adjacently to the sheets. On the top of the paper were my initials: MW.

He tapped his index finger against the top of the sheets and said, "Read and sign; that's all there is to it." He looked away from me, expecting to hear the sound of the ballpoint pen scripting upon the parchment. I could not help but allow regret to come across my spirit. I had been in absolute obedience to a force that had no regard for my well-being. To know that I had fallen so far into his devil's grasp. Life had not been fair nor had it been particularly unfair. I had lived with blind eyes, tired eyes, yet still and ever so, rarely had they found rest. Now that they had, there could be no room made to regress. I bowed my head, and through gritted teeth I hissed, "Did you truly think, that with the tap of your finger, you would simply get that which you have asked?"

"Well, yes. Have I not all the times before?"

I grew frustrated with him; he was both arrogant and my greatest enemy. I could not sit here and pretend that he did not disgust me in every way imaginable. He was a monster hiding behind a face that was not his. Truly, I could no longer be courteous. With purpose I proclaimed in a tone louder than I had used before, "I understand that this must be terribly painful for you, but you have no power over me. No, not anymore—no, not ever again."

He ran his fingers below his jawline and retorted, "Oh, really? Perhaps a little costume change would entice you to listen to me with more attentiveness." He twisted his neck, and it cracked loudly; his body shifted and terribly transformed, shades of black and gray clouding around him. The features on his face slowly contorted into those of another, and then, with a rotation of his head, he asked, "Does this body suit you better?" He mimicked the body of the attractive young man that had stood in the first line in the third spot. My body dramatically tensed, and I could not stomach the idea of something so evil influencing anyone else to act out his malicious biddings. "Now, beautiful girl, love of my life, please sign the sheets, it will only take you a second. I'll let you hold my hand; I know you liked that earlier." This vile monster; I had not approached that man with longing or lust but with compassion and human love. How dare he twist something so wonderful into an act of perversity! He leaned the stolen body over the desk and whispered, "Now that you're a poet, maybe you'll like this." He sat up tall, cleared the young man's throat, and whispered while looking into my eyes, "Be still, my lips will share with you all that my words couldn't." I bolted out of my chair and away from the desk. He then laughed greatly and was again having quite good fun.

Rage swelled, and the fire within lashed at the walls of my spirit. I knew my worth, and for him to demean it in such a belittling manner, I could not accept such burden in my life any longer. I did not attempt to contain the purpose, the fire, and the rage, and to him I yelled, "I know the discomfort of sacrifice; it has left the taste of iron on my tongue, and my heart, by it, it had been left in a reprehensible state."

Leaning forward, he smirked. "Then what is it that you are willing to sacrifice now?"

Heaviness sat on my heart. I lifted my hands and looked down to them, so soft and without scar. They have known no hardship or grueling work, but with them, I can change everything that I touch. I may be small, but the shadow that I cast is large. With hope, with faith, I will do all that my heart asks of me. I reached down toward the bottom of my dress' hemline and began to unravel the fabric that I had knotted. I unwrapped the raw diamond from it and held it in my hand; between my thumb and index finger. I held it to the ceiling then pulled it close to my heart. I approached the desk that he sat leaning upon and placed it before him.

He looked up at me, wearing an expression of uncertainty. I stood before him, next to the wooden chair, and shared, "Though the many might try to shape and mold me, they cannot. This is who I am in my natural shape and form. I found it amongst the rubble, the rubble that I have lived amongst my entire life. I had been there in indifference. And to your eye, you might say that this raw diamond is nothing but a mineral. Allow me to correct you; this is more than the many believe they are. I will not be cut away to resemble that which pleases their eye. I am without luster but with spirit, without acknowledgement but with purpose, and without ability but with willingness. This is an inanimate representation of my spirit, and with my tongue, I give it life. I know who I am, and now, I refuse to be anything else."

He thrashed his body in violence, plodding his foot against the carpeting and slamming his hand against the desk. He looked up at me with the darkest of eyes and said, "This is all you have? Is this all that you offer me? I do not want this! This serves me no purpose—none at all! It is you I need; it is you that I long to drag into the darkness alongside me. Self-worth? Ha! That is nothing but pretty fluffing to lay your worthless heart upon! You are mine, now sign, you wretched, useless girl!"

Two, four, six. I stood strong on confident feet. As the anger grew in him, the fire grew in me. I yelled loudly, "I refuse to sign these sheets! Are you having great fun? Yes? Then so am I!" I grabbed the sheets and profusely tore them apart, rigorously shredded them and tossing the pieces onto the desk and into his face. "How do you answer, demon?"

This demon laughed horridly and mocked me. "How do I plea? Here is my grand confession. Guilty—utterly guilty! I cannot deny this; I am not of sound mind nor can I fathom the extent of heartache I have sown. Actually, easily I can, for I have witnessed all of my tireless work in your life!" he laughed diabolically, growling in enjoyment and insanity. I could no longer bear it; he drove me to madness. What a foul creature! To entertain the fancies of the vulnerable in order to feed his selfish gain. He projected the kindest of sentiments, the loveliest of intentions, but I heeded warning; his fangs were hidden by his purr. Soon he will run away into the darkness, into his forested sanctuary, cold and without company, forever tending to the wounds that I soon intended to inflict upon him.

This man threw his head down while sitting in the high wingback chair; he tightly held on to both arms, and through his snarled mouth came a monstrous howl. I was prepared. He cracked his neck and began to contort just like he had earlier. He laughed and screamed, "You dare deny me after all that I have done? You are mine! You are my prize, my winning game piece! Nothing you could do, no amount of your magic faith or unreciprocated love, will ever change that!" His demon laugh rang against the walls of the room, but no longer—never again—would I fall prey to his demon claws! He bent into an arched position and yelled louder; he craned his neck abnormally to the side as to make it crack, and it loudly did so again. This time was not like the first time. His body changed and mutated into many different bodies; he looked like that of Za'ara, then Maelzer, then like Za'ara again, then like Lou, back into the handsome young man, then the original pale-faced host, and then he looked at me with the face of Fé. It was terrible, and though for a moment, I thought that he had fooled me, that perhaps he had acted as the hosts of each room; I knew that he did not. He preferred high corners and dark spaces; he could not represent what he did not have any great power over.

How long had I allowed him to throw me mentally and emotionally against the pavement, telling me that I had nothing more to offer than my broken bits? Now, with unfailing hope, I saw my potential and wanted nothing more but to piece myself back together again—art, a true masterpiece, and worthy of being hung lovingly upon walls that had always been barren. Long enough had I been made a fool by my unwillingness to name that which had tortured me my entire life. This great darkness of my past was death, and to him I would no longer answer.

It seemed as though the ground beneath my feet had run scarce, and the hope in my heart had grown dim. I wallowed for some time; what was I to do? I feared that the earth would swallow me whole. I remembered everything that I had been through in life. During this journey, faith was uprooting me, pulling me from the rubble that he had convinced me I was doomed to. I should not fear, for the hope in my heart could not wilt or be robbed of me. He was a liar and a thief; for my entire life, I had always known more than poison and thorn. This was the case; the matters of my heart had been clouded by that which he had told me were my own observations, but they were not. My eyes vision had been blurred, and such fog infiltrated my mind and tried to rob my heart of all opportunity.

His body twisted and again became that which I had seen in the alleyway. Wolf-like, a predator, a creature of nocturnal nightmares. He was now that that I always been reluctant to see. Boldly I cried valiant declarations of urgent necessity toward the ambient sense of an omniscient presence; this monster now lurked behind me, the wooden chair in front of me. "I am never truly alone! All my life, all you have done is whisper lies into my life, and I was lost enough to believe them. I am not part of you nor will I be associated with you from this day forward. You have no power over me! None! I reject you, monster! As long as I know you, I will know loneliness, and no longer do I wish to carry such sadness. I do not choose you; I choose life!" I spoke with daggers on my tongue; the thorns of his claws loosened from my flaming heart. I shall not bow; I refuse to bend on knee to those who have no feet to stand on. He who beckons me with devilish lips and poison words—no, I shall protect my heart! He has called me always from the darkness, from his deathly domain, and only from there did he dare to whisper me despair. This demon monster from down below shall not be the death of me. For I have unlimited faith, relentless hope, and undying love; no death shall ever rob me of this. He came from in front of me and leapt toward me; I did not have fear, I just held out my arms, and in this unnatural world, in a way so supernatural, the demon could not touch me. To my touch he roared and fell unto his monster side; he writhed in pain.

I went to him and with my hand touched him as I spoke "Many are worthy, but you, demon, will be forsaken for the rest of eternity." I stretched my arms willingly through the fire of his chest, reaching deeply through his body; the lashes that his searing soul released in a final attempt did not burn or scorch me. And with that of a quick jerk of my arm, he fell to the ground, shuddering and shaking, and as he shook, so did I. He thrashed violently against the ground, jolting and then throwing his body against the mahogany desk. He roared in great pain, and I too cried out. I could not determine what exactly it was running through my blood; it burned like that of a raging fire. It felt like tragedy and tasted of madness. And my eyes, my eyes darted from place to place, so rapidly. My lips moved but said nothing at all. I could not sit, I could not stay still, and my legs wanted to run, but my body was so tired. My face, my face; it lacked color, and the youth that had once graced me no longer kissed my cheek. Difficult times sat at the corner of my eyes and sleepless nights underneath them. If this was poison running through my veins or disease that filled my lungs—I could not determine. This I surely do know: If this continues, then so shall life, and so shall I.

I felt relief overcome my body, and the burden of the great darkness that had intervened throughout my entire life was released from my petite shoulders. Is this sadness because he has left or relief because I have finally let him? The room fell to silence, and I walked across the room to the high wingback chair and rested. Then I heard it; I listened: silence. My heart, this magical melody, it was finally mine—peace. The change was not at all subtle; it could not go without notice. For the first time I stood on ground that did not shake me. How nice it was to walk with absolute purpose and to have love in my heart that had significant meaning. For once, after all this time, my life was of priority, and him, he would be reduced to nothing more but a memory, a lifelong lesson finally learned.

16

I STOOD OVER where the demon had last laid; there were nearly no remains other than the dark ashes that were now on the gray carpet. I breathed in deeply; my blood still ran with high anticipation in expectation of further happening, but none at all was to come. There was only peace now. It had all happened so quickly; my mind, in that moment, gave all that it could, and my heart, so proud of it I was, for it had stood strong when, at another time, I would have not been able to stand at all. My soul, using my spirit as a sword, slew this monster that had brought me so much despair. I almost knew not how to feel; finally, my eyes could rest. They could look upon the world and see all that it had. There was still good; this I knew without doubt. Doubt and fear would always be part of my humanity. To be human is to be flawed, and I was no exception to that rule. I lifted my head and shook off the nerves that had been left from facing a fiend as devilish as the monster who now was only a component of the past. The touch of my skin, the fire within me, captured him; he knew, when he first saw me walk into the room, that I would not fall to his cruel serpent tongue any longer.

The room had not at all changed; there was not a second door to go out through. I looked back at the mahogany desk, back at the raw diamond that represented so much to me. Such thing of beauty, like it, should be not taken but freely given. I closed my eyes. I would leave it; it had already served its grand purpose in my life. I turned away, approaching the door that I had come in through. I walked with a straight spine; my body felt light and free. Peace is not simply granted; it is attained through the many times that we do become lost. I will admit, now that I hold no reservation, that I had always been lost. Now, after winning my freedom from that which had always kept me captive, it is nearly an impossible sensation to describe. Only when we are lost can we be found. I had most certainly been lost, and I had the most certain of hopes that I too had finally been found.

I expected to walk out and see the forest that had been there when I had first walked in, but, no, it was no longer there. What was there instead brought me further comfort; it was the hallway with the extravagant Turkish rug. I skipped some steps forward, so happy and free. My heart wanted to sing praise, to lift the hearts of the many and to encourage those who might not know their way. Never would I guide those who lend me their ear to ill. I would speak with hope and faith, for they had been my saving grace. I looked forward to see where I might go next. In the distance I saw a man. He was sitting on the floor. With caution, I began to walk toward him. This man was not in exultant spirit; he sat in a fetal position on the floor with his head tucked over his legs and both hands holding his legs close. He wore green pants.

It was the handsome man from the atrium, the one who would not look at me. With cautious steps, I approached him, and he did not budge. I stood over him for a moment, hoping that he would lift his head to acknowledge me, but he did no such thing. I empathized for him. Had I not fallen to my knees in tears when I witnessed what they had been demeaned to? I brushed my hair out of my face and wiped underneath my eyes. I sat next to him on the hallway floor, on top of the Turkish rug, shoulder to shoulder. He lifted his face from his arms, which had rested on his bended knee. He stared at me for a moment; the sadness still sat heavily in his pale blue eyes. Then he, without notice, threw his body unto mine and began to weep in my arms; I did not move, I did not say a word, for in that moment, we were no longer strangers.

I placed my hand on his back as to comfort him, but he quickly pulled away from me. He stretched out one leg, keeping the other bent, and wiped his face with his sleeve. He tidied his disheveled hair and ran his fingers across his eyebrows and face. He lifted his chin, facing the wall before him, and without looking at me, he stubbornly spoke, "This is how you come to find me—weeping, releasing the burden of what is to come, of what has been, and that which has been. It did indeed break me. Standing in the same broken place as before, and I am weeping—weeping. Curse this heart of mine, curse this life. Curses. Allow me to weep before time has told this chapter's end; it has been written before, and it will be written again."

Silently I sat next to him, for I had no words to speak. I awkwardly twiddled my thumbs and adjusted my legs. With hesitance on my tongue, I queried, "You were able to leave the atrium?"

With a scoff, he answered, ripping away at his cuticles, "Only after seeing another who had been able to." He lifted his head and quickly glanced at me from his peripheral vision. I turned the other way, not wanting him to see my face. Had I inspired him to find his voice? I had approached him in the atrium and begged of him that he find it in his heart to choose to move forward; could I have really been the one to cause such change? He had carried so much anger, hate; even now, there was what seemed to be bitterness, but perhaps it was only the aftermath of enduring such hardship for so long. Again he glanced at me as though he was expectant of a response. Though now I have learned to not speak with such haste but, instead, with wisdom.

I turned my body so that it would be angled toward him, and he fidgeted in an uncomfortable manner but did not move away. I tilted my head in attempt to find his eyes, and when they did, I asked, "Are you well?"

As though my question triggered an offset emotion, his eyes welled again with sadness. He looked at me then looked to the floor, pulling at its pattered plush. "The thievery of these dark looming days have stolen more than I can bear to part with. Joy, hope, happiness, comfort, trust, faith, love—all consumed by the worrisome winds and jealous rain of the storm of absolution. The heavy torrent of realization weighs so heavily upon me." This man spoke with such poise, with tremendous amounts of insight, but also with unrivaled pain and anguish. When he formed the words that he spoke, it looked as though his expression could not be kept from that of tears. He had been wounded greatly, not on the skin of his body, but on the parts of him that were undoubtedly more important.

He avoided my eyes, and I wondered the reason. Did they tell him more than he could bear to know, or could he simply not stomach the reflection of his own? His pain had become my own, and it was great, but great too was my willingness to share in his burden in hopes of uplifting his spirit. Tenderness left my mouth and fell onto his ear. "Only patience can uphold the promise of tomorrow. Will you not be encouraged and pursue that which you crave? You are worthy, and the best gift you can ever atone yourself with is that of love."

He sighed and leaned the back of his head against the cream wall. He ran his fingers through his hair and then placed his hand on the top of his bent knee and despairingly lamented, "The matters of my heart have been clouded by the observation of my eyes; my mind has been infiltrated by their judgments. They have stolen all chances of happiness. I have seen more than I could ever hope to understand. See, I have come to accept that it is loneliness; I understand but love that I do not."

I could not relate to this man; I've always been intoxicated by the idea of love. How it hurts, how it is sometimes stolen, broken or lost. However, the idea of being in love is, at least in my opinion, much less than actually being in love. One thing was without a doubt: The intricacies of love were much more tender than those that imagination could derive. Only now have I realized this. I had never had a great love before, but now, I have learned to love wholly, unconditionally. Yes, exhaustion had overwhelmed me, as did doubt and fear; how greatly had they plagued me. But now, I will never waver in finding worth in the outpouring of such a wonderful gift as love.

I found my voice and now knew that which I wished to advise him. "Life consists of many mediocrities; love should not be one of them. I understand that pain can be great, but cannot love be all the greater?" Maybe this is it. Maybe all that we love has been poisoned, jeopardized to the fullest extent, or, even worse, we have contorted those things which we say we love. Perhaps we have smothered it, no, maybe we have belittled it to nothingness; have we settled? No. No, now we, we are a stubborn sort, yes, but love, love is a breath of hope, and for so long, we have denied our lungs to experience such true loveliness. He did not speak, breathe, or blink. He stared at the wall in front of me, brought his hand around his ankle, and clasped it. I held on to the piece of fabric that had held the raw diamond and thought it wise to speak again now that I might have obtained the attention of his ear. "Selfish hearts are left in ache; only the brave shall thrive."

He stretched out his other leg and laid it on the ground, extending his calves. "On calloused foot I run; no one is to follow me. I look to the earth, stained in red; that is where I have been, and only from there will I grow. This is where my heart is; though bitter and cold, from this place I shall flourish." I wanted to comfort him, to lend him my hand, but I dare not touch that which was already lost. Exceptions could not be made in regards to the matters of the heart; for this reason both the scorned and the loved found themselves in comparable bouts of heartache. I had already chosen to love myself and to accept the promises of hope and faith, yet so many others looked for the love that they so blatantly denied themselves.

"You will seek and find nothing. Be still; that which is meant for you will fall at your feet. You must first attain peace of self; our self is our greatest asset and our most potent downfall. As for me, I am so consumed by life and the beauty of it, and all I want is more. Through it all my heart has sang; it sails towards the sunrise, and where the light kisses the ocean, that is where I shall find paradise. I believe this with my entire heart, and such a hope I will never forfeit." Such was the truth, my individual truth. I had chosen to abandon all that did not bring me happiness, and he is as I had been—lost. I braided my hair, played with my hands, and asked, "What is your name? Although we are strangers, I feel as though I know you. I had been much like you are now. It has been difficult, but I have come away from the state of heart you are in and have adopted a different mentality."

He lifted his head in exasperation and answered, "Amon. My name is Amon." Amon, a name so lovely to leave my lips and fall upon a man that wishes to know nothing but sadness and self-loathing. I did not know what to do with my body. I stood up. I was so very close to home. The fire still burned within me and gave me purpose; I badly I wanted to move forward, but Amon, though he did not know it yet himself, needed to hear the message that sat on my heart, and with him, I would share it. Although I knew that he was not in a place of acceptance, I spoke nonetheless with charisma, "Amon, you must remember who you are and what you want to represent during this life. There are many fools ten times more foul, but there is hope; you are hope. Do not bend on broken knee. Oh, the terrible things that happen to the many; truly, I weep as well, but when I wake, I know that I work for more than just myself."

Again, he did not look to me but avoided my eyes. I stood above him, but I did not look down on him. He had only been freed from the torment that he had endured by his own choosing. Stubborn man. I spoke love unto him, but he did not wish to hear it. "Amon." He did not respond. Despite his unwillingness, I continued, "Speak, you sit so still. Has life truly stolen your essence? Sleep is sin's solace, slumber a selfish thief; during night's hours you are stripped of sweet dreams, are you not? Rise awake now. Rub the hardships from your swollen eyes. Focus, yes. You are free; now can you see more clearly? Exhale, release the toxins that have poisoned your weary lungs, shrug the burdens off your shoulders—stretch! Rise, reach toward the sun's splendor and touch her flame with eager fingertips; live again. Live. Always live." This time, Amon did look to me. He had vindictiveness in his eyes, yet they had something more.

With passion, he spoke, "Venom has been running though my veins; it brings death to those who evoke fear in me and who bring me pain. There is no doubt that this venom is slowly and surely killing me as well. Pleasure is delayed pain, and pain is wicked pleasure. You are damned; we all are, and the only beautiful miracle left in this life is that we are allowed a voice between the time we are born and the time we die. This I will live by always."

Amon. A man without hope, without faith, so very unwilling to accept all that I tried to share with him. Man is unwilling at times to learn from those who have already undergone the hardships that they themselves will have to experience. To learn from a voice that kindly warns them of what is to come, sometimes the effort is pointless. Had it been me some time ago, it would have also been pointless as well. Some often ask, "Why must I endure such trial and tribulation? For I have done nothing wrong to deserve such hardship. I am good." To that question, still I have no answer, and the closest that I have come to it is this, and this I spoke aloud for Amon to hear: "Always is a promise made by a tongue too coward to taste the fruit of hardships endured. I crave an intimacy of more than tongues and fingertips; such cannot be obtained by the indulgence of the superficial. Such is to be earned by sacrifice. Are you not willing to lose something so small to gain something so large in comparison?"

He laughed in a sarcastic way, in a way that only proved to me that that which I said had effect on him. Such effect might take years to see, but it was not my purpose to change hearts; no, it was my purpose only to plant the seed that they might change it themselves. He had a nearly maddening look to him, much like the one that he had during the storm of absolution. Such madness was reflected in what he said next: "The heavens kiss the horizon, and hell is deep within this rotten ground; yes, this life is purgatory! It is limbo, and your spine will break, bending every which way in the attempt to find your place. Yes, we'll be lost, curses! I prefer the darkness rather than the light that illuminates my sinful nature. Death, I'll take it. It is lovely to be wayward, so nice to be defiant! Tell me, cannot beauty rise even from the filth?" With that said, I understood that I could almost say nothing else that could evoke change in this man. I dreaded that one day he would see me seeing him, for with my whole heart I truly believed that a man was his intentions rather than his downfalls. He had ultimately preferred to dwell within the confines of his denial rather than to confront the unknown that is blind acceptance. In regards to my own heart, I had no doubt that as long as there was life, there was also hope. He was worthy of a beautiful life, of an incredible love. So simply, as I prepared to leave him, I accepted that I was only meant to be a sentence in his story.

And as I turned to walk away from him, I turned to leave him with this thought: "The truth of the matter is that we are human—flawed and freckled with the misconception that beauty lies exclusively upon our flesh. To you I will not lie, for I have lied for far too long and have suffered miserably for it. All that you think you are, you are not; you are more." I left him with a saddened smile, and he looked at me with a furrowed brow.

I nodded my head to him and turned away, and then to me he called and said, "There is one thing that I have no doubt of." I gave him my attention while wearing no expression. "I have no doubt that I will see you in another life."

I closed my eyes, listened to the voice that I had come to trust, and replied, "If that is where your certainty lies, then mine will be there as well. With that being said, see you in another life, Amon." He resumed the posture that I had come to find him in, except now he no longer wept.

He was nothing more than surface and rehearsed depth. We fail to see that which is most clear, and that is the most painful truth for a heart to endure. I knew he ached. And at this time in my life, I have come to understand that love is lost but by two ways. First, by the misconception that the façade of love is love itself. And, second, that emotional degradation is necessary for continuance. By both accounts I have lost, but by both have I also significantly gained. Unconditional love is given in selflessness and taken in selfishness; regardless, both hearts can ultimately become broken, but only one will ever know peace. My purpose, whether derived from a rib, the dirt, or the boot of an enemy, is not lost in translation. Instead, it is unbelievably lost in the chaos of the amazing hurt that this magnificent life can deliver us. This must be the state of his heart: undelivered. The promise, though, at least the one that I understand in faith, is this: that the slain spirit can forever be reborn at sunrise.

Through it all, through the false stops and the untimely disasters; the entire time, purpose has been unraveling the entire time. All the while my doubts and fear only caused my reason for being to become knotted, tangled, and frayed. All for something, all for some unknown reason. A reason—isn't that what we yearn for? A reason, an answer, or a purpose. And we become lost in unaccepted apologies, in unanswered pleas—lost in every heartbroken bellow. Though at times it may not seem as though we are not, we are, undoubtedly, coming all the closer to recognizing everything for what it truly is and so much more. We will come closer to the peace we suffer for. And though sacrifice is not of convenience, it brings us closer to a reason worth suffering for.

17

———— ✦ ————

I DID NOT look back at Amon. If it will be as he said
he believed, then I would see him again. I walked down
the hallway, admiring now, with peace in my heart, all
of its beauty. Here I was, still wondering while wandering,
but no longer lost. With confident steps I walked forward,
and never had I been more pleased. There was miracle to
behold in all that I saw; the lines that were drawn uniquely
on my hand and the way my legs carried the weight of my
petite body. My eyes had been renewed, my spirit and my
heart too. I would soon be home. This I knew, and this I had
all the hope for. I closed my eyes and listened, for I knew I
could be called.

I continued to walk down the hall; there were no doors,
no turns, and no twists. I walked down the straight hallway, my vision broad but my path narrow. Forward I will
continue to go. Now I could not question that which I had
so persistently before. I was thrilled, exhilarated even. I

had become accustomed to routine, to the ordinary, and to what has been deemed as normality. I have lived with blind eyes, tired eyes, yet now only could they know rest. With eyes open, perhaps that is when I had been the most blind, most unaware of what truly has surrounded me throughout my unaccomplished time inhaling selfish amounts of filthy air. I saw everything for what it was: a flower as a flower, a child's playroom for merely a playroom, and a shop for a shop. Seeing the ordinary limited the extraordinary; accepting only the natural left no room for the supernatural. No. I choose to be awake; I choose to be alive. Boldly, fearlessly, I continued toward the end of the hall.

I saw something quickly come into my vision; from around a corner it came running. I shifted my body toward the other side of the hall as to avoid it as it ran along the edge of the wall. I looked down at the direction of my feet, and a mouse scurried by. How strange, just as it had happened in the warehouse. She stopped and turned back at me as though she was reassuring me that the way I went was right and was safe, as though she had made the journey herself and prepared way for me. Excitedly, I ran forward, and on the left of the hallway was a staircase—my staircase. I stood at the foot of the first descending step and looked down; they were comforting and familiar, and I was not at all intimidated. I took my first step. I stepped down and continued to without thinking where I was going or when

I would arrive. Finally, I was standing at the edge of the foot of the stairs; I was home. I dared to look back to see where I had been. It was just a staircase like those that I had climbed many times and time again. It seemed as though I had never been elsewhere, and if I had, it felt as though it had been quite some time long ago.

I stood in a familiar setting. Home. Silence was ever-present, but this did not alarm me. I had come to appreciate silence, for silence was an opportune time to conduct self-evaluation. I turned my body toward my bedroom cautiously, watching my step. I was alone, but I was not lonely. Perhaps this absence of company was necessary. With a tentative sigh, I leaned my head back and stretched. My body was tired, but not due to exertion. No, in fact, from this day forward, I will be resting well. My heart had been transformed, my spirit set on fire, and this life had been given new, renewed perspective. I turned around and looked once again at the staircase; if I walked up once more, would I return to the place of unknown that I had been? I took one step up, leaving the other on the floor of my home. I closed my eyes—no. I had received the gift of having such an experience once; for that, I was thankful, for it has changed me completely.

I turned away now without doubt and fear and went under the archway of my home and toward the restroom. I flipped on the light switch and turned on the water, staring at my face in the mirror while the water ran. My hair, my eyes, and the complexion of my face; nothing had visibly changed, yet the transformation was significant. Bending forward over the sink, I splashed my face with water and let it sit on my skin for a bit. I could nearly hear the sound of the violin playing within my heart, its melody flowing musically through my veins. I closed my eyes and splashed my face once more, wiping away the drops with a towel cloth. Looking at myself, I could not help but to recall all that I had learned from this place that I still had no name to call. It had given me my life back, the life that had been stolen from the darkness that had crippled all that would make me whole since my years of childhood.

For the morning when your mind is still and the flames that ignite your soul are dimmed, take a moment to understand that not all things are earned through blood and tears. Many times, they are, instead, won through patience, that is when you will be set apart from the many. I had often believed that the sharp rise in temperature that moved in my blood was madness when often it was merely that of passion. We are human, faulty in every imaginable way, and we are our only hope for the days to come. All we have is ourselves, our loved ones, faith, love, and the many other wonderful things that we unintentionally take for granted. You are part of something important; let this sink in. Let this information, this known truth, drown out every breathing fear, every seething inhibition, and every senseless doubt. Human acceptance is necessary; self-destruction to gain it is not. You, dearest friend, are a wonder to behold. Do not doubt your worth when blind eyes fail to see it.

Those who see are blind, and the blind believe they see, and so it continues—the deterioration of a nation. Those who reign do nothing, and those who do nothing lose reign, and so it continues—the fall of progression. And those who lash their tongues in vanity drown out those who intend to speak in honesty, and so it continues—the degradation of humanity. If we stopped meeting society's expectations and instead did that which made us feel alive, would not the morning hours be all the more enjoyable? And the nights that you had laid in bed, desperately searching for a comfortable position to hold yourself in, all the more bearable? Conversation has become superficial. I do not want to merely speak pretty candy words; I want to speak in volumes loud enough to evoke change. Change sits at the back of our throats. Ask questions; feed inquiry with personal truths. Being "simply is" will not suffice.

My theory of circumstance, of that which comes to be, does not stem from coincidence but from consciousness. See, words sit on our tongues and, once translated, are given life. Then here lies the most necessary question: What shall you speak into your life? Once spoken, will it be worthwhile? I humbly beg of you, always allow love to roll off your tongue. In my journey to righteousness, I stumbled and landed amongst the wicked; I have seen evil sit on the shoulders of man and whisper despair into their souls. This is the cause of your disease and distress: You open your heart to illness, and with your tongue, hell is given delight. It had been the cause of mine. I find the call of the rooster to be equally as comforting as the cry of the crow; what wakes must one day sleep, but today, I live. I will not be made lost by the lost, and I wonder a great many things, but that which I wonder most often is if all that has come to me has been though chance or by grace. I choose to live by grace. To sleep peacefully for a night is to dream a thousand dreams, and when I wake, I am renewed.

Anywhere else I could go would only leave me longing for the places I had been, for the person I had now been brave enough to become. I had been enlightened; the many could not forcefully remove me from the place in which I had come to find solitude, where I had finally found peace after all the years of agony. It had been as though my insides were set afire, yet no sensation of pain was present. There was no discomfort, no yearning to evade the flames that were presumably swallowing me whole. These flames were not of madness or of ill-want but of passion and purpose. Only if the many were able to steal me away from the dancing light that warmed my aching soul; that is when the heaviness of this reality could suffocate me. I had found refuge in this new place. For the longest time I was unsure of myself, not quite happy and not quite sad. Something was numb, asleep, and whatever it was, it did not want to be bothered. For many years, I had been most fond of sleep, and when sleep did not come, I entertained strangers and needless insecurities, for rest did not privilege the doubtful. The walls of my heart did not need to be broken down by force but by my own willingness; I had been able to do so and not at all on my own. And now, for no particular reason, I have begun to rub the sleep from my eyes, and though my surroundings may become unclear, my path will not. If nothing else, of today, and of this life, I shall ask: What more?